bang

bang

VISIONS BOOK TWO

LISA McMANN

SIMON PULSE

NEW YORK   LONDON   TORONTO   SYDNEY   NEW DELHI

SIMON PULSE

An imprint of Simon & Schuster Children's Publishing Division

1230 Avenue of the Americas, New York, NY 10020

First Simon Pulse hardcover edition October 2013

Copyright © 2013 by Lisa McMann

All rights reserved, including the right of reproduction in whole or in part in any form.

SIMON PULSE and colophon are registered trademarks of Simon & Schuster, Inc.

For information about special discounts for bulk purchases, please contact

Simon & Schuster Special Sales at 1-866-506-1949 or business@simonandschuster.com.

The Simon & Schuster Speakers Bureau can bring authors to your live event.

For more information or to book an event contact the Simon & Schuster Speakers Bureau at 1-866-248-3049 or visit our website at www.simonspeakers.com.

Designed by Mike Rosamilia

The text of this book was set in Janson Text.

Manufactured in the United States of America

2 4 6 8 10 9 7 5 3 1

Library of Congress Cataloging-in-Publication Data

McMann, Lisa.

Bang / by Lisa McMann. — 1st Simon Pulse hardcover ed.

p. cm. — (Visions ; bk. 2)

Summary: "A teen who used to see a vision of a crash must help her boyfriend as he is now seeing a vision of a school shooting"— Provided by publisher.

[1. Visions—Fiction. 2. Supernatural—Fiction. 3. Love—Fiction. 4. Family problems—Fiction. 5. School shootings—Fiction. 6. Schools—Fiction. 7. Chicago (Ill.)—Fiction.] I. Title. PZ7.M478757Ban 2013 [Fic]—dc23 2012028658

ISBN 978-1-4424-6625-8

ISBN 978-1-4424-6629-6 (eBook)

To awesome green-eyed boys everywhere

bang

bang.

One

It's been over a week since Sawyer kissed me and told me *he* was seeing a vision now, and it's all I can think about. I can't wait to get out of this apartment, which I am tethered to until Monday—that's when the doc said my internal injuries will be healed enough so I can go to school again. My older brother and best friend, Trey, has been great, of course, slipping notes to Sawyer for me and delivering replies back to me. But for some reason Sawyer won't explain his vision on paper. "It's too . . . frightening. Too gruesome. Too . . . everything," he wrote.

And me? I'm sick about it.

Absolutely sick.

Because it's my fault. I was so relieved when my vision ended—no more snowplow crashing and exploding into

Angotti's restaurant, no more body bags in the snow, no more Sawyer's dead face. After weeks of that stupid vision taunting me, and after nearly getting killed because of it, I was naive enough to think it was all over and I'd get to live a happy life. Relatively, anyway. Under the current parental circumstances, that is.

But then, once I got home from the hospital, Sawyer sent me that note. He had to see me, he said. That night, 2:00 a.m. And I wanted to see him, too. I eased my broken body down the stairs and we stood in the snowdrift surrounded by breathy clouds and he kissed me, and I kissed him back, and it was the most weirdly amazing feeling. . . .

And then the amazingness of my first kiss was over. He pulled away and looked at me, his gorgeous green eyes filled with fear, and his voice shook. *You know that billboard?*

Those words haunt me.

Obviously I was not only psychotic enough to *have* a vision, but I managed to give the stupid vision disease to the one person I was trying to save.

It's beyond horrifying, sitting here knowing he must be experiencing the worst kind of frustration and pressure to act on the vision and—Did he say "gruesome"?

Let me say it one more time. Sick. That is what I am.

And so very sorry.

I rack my brain trying to figure out how this could have happened. Was it because he hugged me on the street the night before? Because he held my hand afterward in the hospital? Maybe there's some kind of physical transference going on. I have no idea.

I have done something horrible to the boy I love, and I don't know how to stop it.

All I know is that I need to get out of this hoardhole before I *lose my mind*.

Oh, wait.

Two

Finally. School.

I get up a little earlier than Trey and my younger sister, Rowan, partly because my eyes fly open at five thirty in anticipation of seeing Sawyer, and partly because it takes me a little longer to get my makeup on with the half-arm cast wrapping around the base of my thumb.

I sneak out of the bedroom I share with Rowan, plastic-wrap my cast, and grab a shower, then try to do something with my hair—the bedhead look was fun for a while but, well, you know.

At six, like clockwork, I hear two doors open almost simultaneously, and then the precarious race to the bathroom as Trey and Rowan dodge my father's hoards of junk that line the hallway. I open the door a crack and Trey bursts in.

"Dang it," Rowan mutters from somewhere behind him.

"Look at you, hot girl," Trey says, keeping his frame in the doorway so Rowan can't sneak past.

"Yeah?" I say, biting my lip. I freaking love my brother. Love him to death.

"You know you're going to get mobbed, you big hero."

Rowan pokes Trey in the back. "Come *on*," she whispers, not wanting to wake our parents. "Either let me in or get your own butt in there."

"Whatever happened to sweet morning Rowan?" I ask Trey like she's not there.

He shrugs.

"Sweet morning Rowan died looking at your face," Rowan mutters. She gives up and goes to the kitchen.

I snicker and do a final inspection. My black eye has healed, my various stitches have been removed, and my hair actually does look kind of awesome. My arm doesn't hurt anymore. My insides are feeling pretty good too, though I'm not allowed to drive quite yet after the surgery. Only my stubborn left thigh remains a beastly mottled yellow-green, having abandoned black, blue, and purple as the weeks passed. It still hurts to press on it, but at least no one can see the bruise under my clothes. And hopefully I'll have this arm cast off in a few weeks.

As I slip out of Trey's way, I stop. "Any chance we can leave a few minutes early?"

"If you get out of here already," Trey says.

"I'm gone." I step into the hallway with a grin and he closes the door in my face.

In the kitchen, Rowan has her head in the sink and the faucet extended. She's washing her hair like it's frisée lettuce.

"Gross," I say. "Getting your hair germs all over Mom's nice clean sink."

"Listen, you wanna know what goes in here?" comes her muffled reply as she turns the water off and replaces the faucet. "The juice of meat. I'm telling you right now this sink is freaking overjoyed to see my awesome hair in it."

Did I mention I adore my sister, too?

I grab breakfast while she wraps her head in a towel and starts doing her makeup in the reflection of the kitchen window. "We're leaving a little early today," I tell her.

"I figured," she says, the cap of her eyeliner pencil in her mouth. Her head towel falls to the floor and her long auburn hair unfurls.

"You going to talk to Charlie today?" I bite a hunk off some cardboard-tasting health bar rip-off and wrinkle my nose. Chew it anyway. I'm too nervous to eat but I know I need something.

"Yep." She starts working a wide-toothed comb

through her hair, and when it sticks, she looks around the kitchen with a scowl until her eyes land on the carafe of olive oil. "Aha," she says, and puts a few drops into the palm of her hand and works it into the knot.

"Resourceful," I say.

Charlie is Rowan's boyfriend. He lives in New York. They met at soccer camp, and now they video chat every day from school during Rowan's study hall. "So everything is good with you two?" I look around, unsettled. Anxious. I got up way too early.

"Yep," she says again, and then gets a hair dryer, plugs it in, and turns it on.

I drum my fingers on a stack of crap on the table and glance at the clock. "Okay, then."

My stomach flips as I think about school. I don't want to be a hero. I don't want to be noticed by anybody. It's embarrassing. And I'm so beyond what happened when Trey and I barreled into that snowplow to keep it from hitting Angotti's Trattoria. Ever since Sawyer told me he's been having a vision now too, I haven't been able to stop worrying about him, and about what horrible thing he's going to be forced to go through.

My chest aches thinking about it. It was the worst time of my life. I felt so alone. "Poor Sawyer," I murmur.

"Yeah, poor guy. He's really dreading seeing you," Trey says sarcastically from behind me.

Rowan catches sight of her bathroom opportunity, yanks the hair dryer cord from the outlet, and runs for it.

I smirk at Trey. He is so awesome that he actually believed me when I told him what was happening to me—after a while, anyway. Like, thirty very important seconds before the crash happened.

But he doesn't know about Sawyer.

Three

We all climb into the pizza delivery car since there's no longer a giant truck o' balls—I totaled the sucker.

Luckily, har har, the insurance money is going to provide us with a new one. Dad's having the old balls fixed and mounted. Apparently they snapped off pretty cleanly in the crash and didn't get banged too hard (dot-com), thanks to the snow.

Trey drives, Rowan's in the back, and I'm riding shotgun, peering out the windshield as a flurry of snow buzzes around the car. I can't concentrate on anything, but I stare at a vocab worksheet for a test I've been told we're having today.

I glance up as we pass the infamous billboard, and

there's Jose Cuervo, thank the dogs. I wonder for the millionth time what Sawyer sees.

As we near school, my right leg starts jiggling and I put my vocab paper away. It's useless to do anything. Out of habit, I reach for my phone, but of course it's not there—it was pulverized in the crash and so far my parents haven't been too keen on replacing it. Trey glances at me as we pull into the parking lot. "You okay?" he asks.

I let out a little huff of breath. "I think so. It's weird."

"Nervous?"

"I—I guess. I've been gone a long time." The truth is, I'm nervous because Sawyer and I never talked about what would happen at school. Like, are we a couple? Or are we being secretive so nobody tells our parents? Or . . . am I not cool enough for his friends?

I hate that I just had that last thought. What the crap happened to turn me into an insecure loser? I was doing so well there for a while, back when I accepted the fact that I was a total psycho. Amazing how freeing that was. I take a few deep breaths and find that old crazy confidence as Trey parks and turns off the car, and then I ease out, making sure I move carefully. I don't want to overdo it or anything, or I'll get stuck back home again.

"Don't worry, Jules," Rowan says, surprising me because I thought she was listening to her music all this time. "We got your back."

Trey takes my backpack since I'm not allowed to lift more than, like, twenty pounds for another week or so, and the backpack, with a few weeks' worth of work in it, officially weighs forty-seven tons. And then we walk into school. The three of us together in a line, like we're the friggin' Avengers, gonna take somebody down.

I stare straight ahead, Trey on my left, Rowan on my right, feeling totally badass despite my nerves. We get a few glances, a few people shrugging in our direction or outright pointing at us. At me. We even get a smattering of applause from some of Rowan's ninth-grade friends at their lockers, and everybody's saying hi to Trey and me like it's opposite day here in Chicagoland. I ease my way up the half-dozen steps to the sophomore hallway, not able to take stairs at full stride quite yet, using the handrail to help. And then we're nearing my locker and I have to work hard not to strain to look for Sawyer. I want *him* to look for *me*. That's how this is going to go. I just decided.

"That's good, you guys," I say, and I hate that I'm a little winded. I think that's the longest distance I've gone in one stretch in a while. "I got this."

Trey sets my overladen backpack inside my locker and gives me a quick grin as he leaves. "See you at lunch."

Rowan hangs around for a second like she doesn't want to leave. "You sure you're good?"

I nod. "Sure. Say hey to Charlie for me and I'll see you

after at the balls. Dot-com." I pause, realizing what I just said, and then we both make faces. "At the car, I mean."

"Okay. See ya." She heads back toward her hallway.

I turn to my locker to pull out a few books as the guy whose locker is next to mine says, "Hey, Jules. Welcome back."

We've barely spoken before. This is weird.

"Thanks," I say, suddenly shy. I take my coat off and go to hang it up, when I hear the voice that makes my thighs quake.

"Catch you later, guys. Hey, Jules."

Before I can turn around, he's turning me around, and then his gentle arms are hugging me, lifting my feet off the ground. Holding me. Right here in public. I let my coat fall from my fingers and I wrap my arms—cast and all—around his neck like it's the most natural thing for me to do in the middle of a crowded high school hallway.

"I missed you so much," he whispers into my hair, and the world goes quiet around us. My body pulses with energy and I can feel his warmth seeping into me.

I close my eyes and breathe, wishing everybody would just disappear.

He sets me back down and I look at his face for the first time in what seems like forever. He smooths my static hair and keeps a hand on my shoulder. The corner of his mouth turns up on one side, just the way I like it. But his eyes are tired.

"I missed you too," I say in a quiet voice, suddenly hyperaware of people staring at us, my former friend Roxie and her BFF Sarah among them. Which makes me feel really awkward, so I try to pretend they're not there.

He observes the cast on my arm and smooths a thumb under the eye that used to be black. "Nice," he says. He glances over one shoulder, then the other, gets a goofy smile on his face, and moistens his lips. "I really want to kiss you," he says quietly near my ear. But I think we're being cautious, or else he spotted a teacher, because instead of kissing me he just runs his thumb across my lips and looks at me so longingly it hurts.

"Dang," I say, a little breathless. "Where's a stupid playground when you need one? This, uh, environment feels . . . awkward."

"I wanna be your playground," he says in my ear, and I feel the heat rushing to my face. I can see he's just messing around, flirting, but he stays close, like he can't stand to have much space between us, and I like him there.

"Rowr." I grin, but I'm preoccupied, searching his eyes, and the grin falls away. As he watches me watch him, his face changes, like he can read the question in my mind.

"About that," he says, as if we started the conversation already. "I desperately, *desperately* need to see you alone." And even though his eyes are hungry, this is different.

"I know." I've been thinking about this already. "Mr. Polselli is on parking-lot duty during lunch on Mondays. He'll let me eat in his room. I'll claim I need your help because of the cast."

"You're brilliant," he says with a breath that trickles down my neck. "I'm sorry I haven't told you—I'll explain everything, it's just—"

I press a finger to his lips and watch his eyelids droop halfway in response. "I get it," I tell him, and reluctantly pull my finger away when the bell rings.

His gaze lingers and burns. "See you at lunch," he says. "I'll bring two trays and meet you there."

When he disappears in the crowd, I turn back toward my open locker and stare into it, dazed. *Holy big sizzle, Demarco.* Is it hot in here or is it just my gorgeous boyfriend? At this rate, we'll have, like, nine babies by the end of our senior year.

Four

Before lunch I dodge strangers and classmates trying to talk to me, which is absolutely the weirdest experience of my school life, and find Trey to let him know I'm going to have a private lunch with Sawyer, so I'll see him in art class.

He smirks. "Tell the two-timing lunch whore I said hey."

"I will kiss him for you," I say, and then I add, "I hope, anyway." But Trey has moved on with the hallway traffic.

I slip into Mr. Polselli's empty room, sit at a desk, and wait, forcing myself to work on a math assignment. When the door opens, I look up and my smile freezes on my face. Not only is it Sawyer with two lunch trays, but Roxie and BFF Sarah are with him, apparently there to open the door.

Sawyer and Roxie are laughing at BFF Sarah, who rants about something, and all I can think about is how I want them gone.

"Oh. Hi, Julia," Roxie says to me, like she didn't expect to see me. "Thanks for saving our favorite restaurant."

I stare at her, wondering if she's really that rude that she values the restaurant over the human lives—Sawyer's life—or if she's just stupid. But new Jules isn't going to smile and walk away. "Wow. Did you really just say that?" I say. I glance at Sawyer, who looks almost as offended as I feel.

Roxie looks confused. "Yeah, did you not just hear me?"

BFF Sarah's lack of greeting brings frostiness to the air. She's probably still peeved about the V-Day decorations I knocked out of her hands.

"Okay, well, thanks for the help," Sawyer says pointedly to them. He sets a tray on my desk and then sits down at the one next to me. "Can you close the door on the way out?"

Roxie's hands go to her hips, and her lips part as if to protest, but Sawyer ignores them both. He reaches out and strokes my shoulder. "How's it going so far? You taking it easy?"

BFF Sarah rolls her eyes, mutters, "Whatever," and walks out the door, then stands in the hallway waiting for Roxie.

"It's good," I say. My mouth has gone completely dry from the tension.

Finally Roxie turns and leaves, letting the door close hard behind her.

I press my lips together and form a smile. "That went well."

"I don't want to talk about them," Sawyer says. He leans toward me and slides a warm hand along my cheek, sinking his fingers into my hair and pulling me close. I close my eyes and our mouths meet. Blood pounds through his fingers and lips, echoing in my ears. My head spins with all kinds of surprising thoughts as my fingers explore his shoulders through his shirt. Thoughts like how I saw his bare, bony torso once when the boys played shirts and skins in fifth grade, and now, even though he's still lean, his sinewy arms and back are roped with muscle, and I really want to see that chest once more.

When I come to my senses and realize the trouble we'll be in if Mr. Polselli walks in right now, I reluctantly pull back, a little breathless.

Sawyer opens his eyes. "I've been waiting a long time for that." He pulls his fingers from my hair and smooths it back into place.

"Tell me about it," I say, and then I get a little shy, because here we are, in school, having hardly spoken to each other for years, and now we're making out. In a way everything with Sawyer is so new and raw, but in another way, it feels like the most natural progression. We were so close before, and I still feel like I *know* him, you know?

"So . . . ," I say, still tasting him on my lips. "Are we, like, going public with this? And if so, is that a good idea?"

He grins. "I've been thinking about that, and you know, Jules, I don't want to hide it. But it's up to you. If you feel like we need to because of your parents, I totally understand. Obviously."

"What about your parents and your grandfather?"

Sawyer's face sets. "Like I said in the hospital, I'm done playing along with their stupid game."

"But—" Impulsively I reach out and brush my fingers across his cheekbone, imagining his grandfather beating him, and let my hand rest on his arm.

"He can't hurt me anymore," he says in a quiet voice, and I feel his biceps twitch through his sleeve. "Besides, I've got other shit to worry about."

"Aaand there's that," I murmur, and turn to our lunch trays. I grab a few carrot sticks and blush when I bite down and they explode like firecrackers in the quiet room. "Ready to tell me?"

Sawyer's eyes close and he lets out a resigned breath. He shakes his head the slightest bit, and then he opens his eyes and stares at the whiteboard in front of us. "I'm not exactly sure how to explain this," he says. "I mean, I'm not sure what happened with you or how you saw your . . . your clues, or whatever. . . ." He looks at me for help, and I realize I've never actually had a chance to describe to him what happened to me—I'd only told him that I saw a vision of a truck hitting his restaurant and exploding.

"The first time was at the movies," I say. "Before the previews, when they have that 'Turn off your cell phones' ad. I saw a few seconds of the snowplow careening over the curb, smashing into your restaurant, and exploding. There was never any sound, just the picture. And then the Jose Cuervo billboard—it had a still shot of the truck explosion." I hesitate as I relive it, having tried so hard to block it out. "Then I saw it on TV—and there was a new part added. Nine body bags in the snow. One of them was open, showing a face."

I drop my head into my hand, not wanting to say the next part.

"A face?" he asks.

I nod and whisper, "Your face."

He is quiet for a long minute. Then he stands up and shoves his desk right up to mine, moving our uneaten food to a different desk. He sits back down and we drape our arms around each other as I tell him the rest of it. I tell him about the gripping fear when I found out Angotti's was closed that one Saturday night. All the times I drove past his restaurant to check if it was still there. The way

I studied the scenes and tried to figure things out by the snow levels on the street. The vision's growing frequency, intensity, and urgency until almost every place I looked was covered in the scene being played out. And my weird phone calls and visits to him, knowing there was no way he'd believe me, but having to do something about it.

When I finish, he nods slowly. And then he says, "Mine has sound. But not voices or street sounds or background noises. Eleven sounds, to be exact. All the same." He makes a gun with his finger and thumb and points it at Mr. Polselli's papier-mâché bust of Ivan Pavlov. "Bang."

Five

My hand goes to my mouth. "A shooting?" I whisper.

His mouth twitches. "A school shooting."

"Oh my God." I look around the room as the shock of it hits home. "What, here? Our school?"

His Adam's apple bobs and his eyes turn desperate. "I don't know, Jules. I can't tell where it is."

"Tell me everything you can think of."

"At first it was so quick I missed it. I remember thinking, 'Wait, what just happened?' and then brushing it off as me being tired. But then I started catching a glimpse of something out of the corner of my eye in the restaurant window, like there was a person standing there on the other side with his arms raised straight out, but whenever I'd look full on, he was gone."

I rest my head against his shoulder and stay quiet, not wanting to interrupt.

"The next thing was the billboard. A still picture of a figure, arms raised and pointing straight ahead, firing a gun—muzzle flash and everything."

I frown. "Muzzle flash?"

"When you pull the trigger of a gun, it ignites gunpowder, which explodes, pushing the bullet out. There's a little flash of fire that comes out the barrel, but you can't usually see it."

"Why not?"

He shrugs and thinks about that for a minute. "Partly because it happens really fast. But also because there's usually too much natural light, I guess."

"Ah. So this vision of yours—it happens at night?"

He frowns. "Huh," he says, and then he looks at me. "Maybe. You're good at this."

I give a sordid laugh. "Forced on-the-job training makes you an expert in a hurry. You'll learn, kid. Stick with me."

"No worries there," he says, looking slightly relieved.

"So you're only seeing stills? And you hear gunfire from them?"

"No, no sound from the stills. We have TVs in the restaurant bar, and not long after the billboard incident, when I was busing a table, I glanced at it and saw the same figure—person with a gun, arms outstretched, and he was stepping backward and swinging the gun wide, like he was feeling threatened. I stopped working and stared at it, and then the gunshots exploded in my head and I dropped my tray."

I wince. "Was it dark?"

He hesitates. "Well, I could see the guy. Not his face— he was turned away. And I could see, um, bodies. But it wasn't sunny or bright in there or anything."

I knit my brows, thinking. "How do you know this guy is at a school?"

"I don't know—it just looked like a school. It was all really fast—it felt . . . schoolish."

"Yeah, okay," I say, trying not to sound impatient. I remember how many hundreds of times I had to see mine before I caught everything. "You'll get more information eventually."

Just then somebody opens the door, sees us, and says, "Oops!" really loudly. I can hear people swarming the hallways. The dude closes the door again, and I glance at the clock. Four minutes until lunch is over.

Sawyer follows my gaze. "That went way too fast," he says, getting up. He picks up the food trays and stacks one on top of the other like the server pro that he is, balancing them with one hand. "I guess I should get these back to the kitchen."

I stand up too, grabbing a roll from the top tray and pulling a hunk off. "You should try to eat something," I say. "You're going to need the energy."

He gives me a weary smile. "Does that mean it only gets worse from here?"

I nod, taking a bite of the roll.

"And it doesn't end until . . . ?"

I swallow. "Until it's over."

We walk to the door and he pauses. "Wait a sec." With his free hand he reaches into his pocket. "I hope this isn't weird," he says, "and you can say no and I won't be offended or anything, but I can't stand not being able to talk to you, especially with . . . *this* thing going on." He pulls out a cell phone and hands it to me. "It's just one of those cheap prepaid ones. No frills. Phone only."

I take it, and it feels like I just got out of jail. "You are brilliant," I say, turning it over in my hand, and then I look up at him and my heart swishes. "Thank you."

"Don't get caught."

"I won't." I shove the phone into my pocket and reach up, thumbing the corner of his mouth until he gives me the smile I love. "I'll call you tonight." It's amazing how nice it feels to be able to say that.

He hesitates, his hand on the doorknob. "Jules?"

I look at him.

"In the vision, I don't see any faces I know."

"Oh." I'm not sure what he's trying to say. "Okay, well, that's good, right?"

But that's not what he means. He hesitates, and then he squeezes his eyes shut like he's making the hardest decision of his life and says, "I was kind of wondering what happens if I don't want to do this."

Six

The bell rings before I can answer, and besides, the question is too much to absorb in ten seconds, so we say a hasty good-bye. All afternoon I think about what he said. And I wonder. If he doesn't know or care about any of the people in the vision, does he have to do something? Is he legally obligated to do something? What about, like, morally?

My guess is that my vision probably would have gone away whether I saved people or not, but I didn't know that back then. Does that change anything? I go back in time in my mind. If I knew that the vision would stop pounding me at every turn if I only waited long enough, would I have done what I did?

That one's not hard. Sure I would have, because of

Sawyer's dead face in the body bag. But then I wonder how I would have looked at it had it been a stranger's face. If every part of the vision stayed the same except Sawyer wasn't going to be hurt or killed, would I have done what I did?

Not quite as simple, but the answer is still yes, because it was Sawyer's family business, and chances were good that some family members filled the other body bags. And as much as we both are disgusted by our parents' behavior—and I'm not talking just my dad's affair with Sawyer's mom, but also the ridiculous rivalry over a stupid sauce recipe—that doesn't mean we want them to die, and I wouldn't want Sawyer to go through that pain.

But what if I knew back then what I know now, and it *wasn't* Angotti's restaurant but some other restaurant somewhere else? If I knew that the visions would get worse and become insane, but I knew that it would end as soon as the crash was over, would I still risk my life to save those people?

I don't think I know the answer.

In the evening, while everybody's still down in the restaurant and I'm stuck doing mountains of worksheets and make-up quizzes that didn't come home with one of the sibs, my mind wanders to it again. I pull out the cell phone, wondering if Sawyer is working, wondering if he's slammed or if he maybe has time to talk.

I start pressing the numbers I know by heart but hardly ever get to use thanks to my father, and the phone's address book recognizes them and brings up Sawyer's name with a <3 next to it. I smile and look at it for a minute, and then I press the call button. It rings a few times, and I cringe. He's probably busy.

"Hey," comes his breathless voice.

Why is it that every time I talk to him I feel like my brain won't work? It takes me a full second to form the word "Hi" in response. "Are you slammed?"

"Nope," he says. "I just got back to the car. Delivered my last pizza for the night. How's your new phone?"

"Love it," I say. Love *you*. "Everybody else is still downstairs, but if I hang up quickly, you'll know why."

"I will always assume a quick click means the proprietors are coming, and not that you're mad or something," he teases.

"Oh, I'll let you know if I'm mad."

There's a smile in his voice. "I do not doubt that. As long as every now and then you still drag me out of bed in the middle of the night to tell me you're sorry I'm going to die, and tell me that you . . ."

He doesn't say it.

I don't know what to say.

When you tell a guy you love him before you're in a relationship with him, does it mean love love? Or just

love? And what words do you use *after* you start the relationship? You can't say "I love you" after a first kiss, I don't
care who it's with. That screams of one of those crash-and-
burn relationships half the school is in. I think I have to go
back to saying "like." For a while, at least.

"Anyway," he says in the awkward pause.

"Anyway," I agree. "So, um, I thought about your
question."

"Me too."

"I guess all I can say is that I don't think you have to
risk your life for strangers." And I stop there, even though
there's so much more I have to say. And want to say.

He's quiet for a long moment. "What do you think will
happen if I don't try to save them?"

"The vision will get stronger and more frequent, and
you'll see it everywhere. You might not be able to drive—I
was really struggling there at the end."

"I'm so sorry—"

"Don't. It's really okay. I never expected you to believe
me." I pause, listening for footsteps on the stairs, but all is
quiet. "The main thing you need to get you through it is
to remember it'll end eventually."

"How do you know that for sure—that it'll end?"

His question stops me. "Um . . . because it ended for
me?" I say weakly.

"Yeah, but you did what it wanted you to do," he says.

"Will my vision still end if I don't do what it wants?"

"I—I guess I don't actually know." I think about it, wondering if I'd still be tormented by the vision today if I hadn't stopped the crash. If I'd have to look at Sawyer's dead face in the body bag until the end of time. And for whatever reason, I think about my dad, and his own apparently tormented life. But Sawyer interrupts my thoughts.

"It's getting worse," he says. "As I'm driving around doing deliveries, it's showing up on street signs."

I frown. "Any new scenes?"

"Not so far. I'm going to try to watch some TV tonight to see if the vision shows up there. Try the rewind/slow motion thing like you said."

I feel helpless. I sigh heavily and say, "I'm just so sorry about this."

"Yeah, well, I blame you, of course."

I afford a small smile, but I can't help it. I feel responsible. This is happening because of me, and it's, like, bodies and bodies—eleven gunshots? Holy shit. "So . . . you aren't going to try to stop the shooting, then?" The words come out strained, because I've already made my decision on what has to happen if he decides not to save anyone. I'm going to have to save them myself.

He's quiet. "Jules," he says finally, sounding a little hurt. "Do you really think I could do that? I volunteer at the freaking Humane Society, you know. How could

I possibly not try to save eleven people from some crazy gunman?"

My heart floods with relief. "I didn't think you would—or could. I just didn't want you to think I'd blame you for hoping to try and make it go away."

"Well," he says, "whatever controls this vision thing sure knows how to pick the right people to get the job done."

I hear a door shut at the bottom of the stairs and my heart races. "Gotta go," I say in a hushed whisper. "But I'm with you on this."

"Thank dog for that," he says, and we hang up.

Eleven fucking gunshots. And his vision is getting worse. I feel like I'm going to puke. All I know is that we gotta get moving on this thing. Now.

Seven

Mr. Polselli is back in his room at lunch, so Sawyer and I eat in the caf the rest of the week with Trey, but we don't talk about the visions. Too many people around. There are a few fleeting moments at my locker and a few short phone conversations, but as the week progresses I get more and more stressed out by the fact that I barely get a chance to see Sawyer, much less talk about what he's going through.

Add to that, I'm feeling guilty about still not going back to work. Plus I'm broke. And the sooner I get working, the sooner I'll be able to do deliveries again now that I'm allowed to drive, which means I'll be ungrounded and I'll get a real cell phone that can do more than just make phone calls, and maybe Sawyer and I can arrange a few clandestine meetings. Not to mention Rowan's been working her face off covering for me. So I ease back into the work scene.

"It's just like old times," Trey says as we three head downstairs to the restaurant together Friday after school. Rowan is in a good mood too—she only has to get us through the dinner rush and make sure I'm cool with everything before she gets the night off to do who knows what.

And it's pretty easy rolling back into it. My body gets tired a little sooner than it used to, and I'm not quite as fast as I'd like to be, but the cast doesn't really get in the way too much and it's actually getting me some pretty nice pity tips.

Trey is out most of the night with deliveries while Mom and I cover the tables and Aunt Mary works front of house. Dad's having one of his depression days and hasn't shown his face, which is actually kind of nice since we really aren't talking right now.

In a lull, Mom joins me in prep and we roll silverware.

"Keeping up all right?" she asks.

"Yep," I say.

"Good."

It's awkward between us, too. Ever since before the crash, I've thought Mom wanted to sort of confide in me—she did already, a little, when she told me she knew it wasn't easy saying good-bye to an Angotti, and she wasn't talking about herself. But she doesn't know I know about Dad's affair.

And the weird thing is, I don't know what to do. Like now, we could talk if she wants to, I guess. "How's everything going for you?" I ask. And I realize I never ask her this.

She tilts her head and smiles, seemingly pleased that I have put aside my selfish ways for the first time ever. "Not bad," she says. "Old Mr. Moretti pinched my butt again. I think he's going senile."

"Maybe you're just a hottie," I say, grinning. "He never does that to me."

"He'd better not or he won't know what hit him. I don't want you girls waiting on him." She pauses and lightens up again. "If he weren't senile I'd kick him out. But I haven't been pinched in public since the nineties on the L." She says it wistfully.

"Mom," I say. I don't want to know about her glory days or whatever. Then I think about it. "You know, that's really kind of sad. You should get pinched at least once a week."

"You'd think," she mutters, and then she laughs and tosses her hair a little.

I set down a roll of silverware and glance at her. "How's Dad these days?" I ask, tentative. "Any chance he's ready to unground me yet?"

She laughs again.

"I'm seriously asking you."

She pulls in a breath and sighs, and then she shakes her head a little, grabbing a new package of napkins and slicing the wrapper open with a little retractable utility blade she keeps in her apron. "Julia," she says, turning to me, "it's complicated. And no, I don't see you getting ungrounded anytime soon."

I scowl and glance at my lingering guests. "What's so complicated? You guys are—" I clamp my mouth shut, knowing pointing fingers isn't going to get me anywhere, especially when I think Mom might be on my side. "Sorry. It's just frustrating. I don't feel like I'm doing anything wrong."

"Whoa. Seriously? Leaving work, stealing the meatball truck and wrecking it, not to mention yourself, seeing a guy you are forbidden to see, and sneaking around with him at two in the morning?"

I try to breathe. "I wouldn't have to sneak if you guys weren't so—" *Ugh.* I catch myself again. "Look," I say as a customer catches my eye, "I just think the Angotti-Demarco rivalry is so . . . Middle Ages. Or whatever. Shakespearean. Overdramatic. It's ridiculous that Dad can't get over it."

"It would have been a lot of money," Mom says.

"Only if Dad had the drive to actually manufacture

and sell the stinking sauce, like Fortuno did." I pause. "Or do you mean the money you would have gotten from suing the Angottis over it?" I set down my last roll of silverware hard. "Customer," I say as I walk off, so she doesn't think I'm stomping away mad.

"Who knows? Ask your father," she mutters under her breath. I don't think she expected me to hear that.

Eight

The weekend is endless. I'm working when Sawyer's off, he's working or volunteering when I'm off, and we don't even manage to connect for a quick phone call. I hate this. Hate not knowing what's going on, hate that hours and days are ticking away and we're not doing anything. I'm worried as hell.

The phone vibrating in my hand wakes me at two in the morning. It takes me a second to pull out of my dream and figure out what's happening. I sit up on one elbow and answer it.

"Hey, are you okay?" I whisper, my voice full of sleep and air.

He doesn't answer for a second, and I think maybe it's an accidental rolled-over-on-his-phone-in-the-night call.

But then he says in a quiet voice, "Jules, I'm—I'm just—I'm freaking out a little."

I glance at Rowan and she hasn't even moved. "What's happening?" I turn my face away from the door, as if that'll keep my whispers from slipping under it.

"It's, well, I had a chance to watch the vision on TV a few times. Like fifty, I mean, and it's—" I can hear the whir of anxiety in his voice notching up. He takes a breath. "It's really horrible. It almost made me puke. I swear."

I press my lids shut with my fingertips. "Oh, God," I say. There are no other words. "Are you taking notes? Writing it all down?"

"Yeah. Some."

I think I hear a creak of the hallway floor, but it's nothing. I pull the blankets over my head. "What can I do? How can I help you?"

I hear the tightness in his throat as he swallows hard, hear the air rush from his nostrils into the phone, a tiny blast of emotion. And then it comes again, and he doesn't speak, and I know he's trying to hold it together.

"Shit, I remember this," I say. My gut twists. "I know how tough it is." I cringe, thinking I sound like a condescending jerk when what I really mean to say is, *It's okay to cry with me.*

It turns out he doesn't need my permission. After a few minutes of him in not-quite-silent sobs and me staring into the caverns of my blankets, wishing I could be with him, remembering and remembering, he blows out a breath and says, "I don't think I can do this alone."

"You're not alone, Sawyer."

His silence tells me he feels otherwise, and suddenly I'm furious. Not at him. At my parents, and at his parents. And at the ridiculousness of this. I can't see or help my friend, my boyfriend, because of something gross my father did.

"This is nuts," I mutter, throwing my blankets off and sitting up on the side of the bed. I can hardly contain the surprise tsunami of anger that floods me. "Where are you?"

"In my room."

"Do you want me to come over?" I cringe again, imagining the trouble I could get into, but the anger is bigger than that fear, and the boy across town is more important than the man in the next room.

"No. I mean yes, of course, obviously. But no. I'm okay now, and we don't need any more trouble with the proprietors. I'm just glad . . ." He trails off for a moment, and his voice goes soft. "I'm just glad you answered. And that you're there."

I can hardly stand it. "I'm here. We'll figure out something. I can't take this either. I need more than a few minutes at my locker with you." I don't think I would have said that if it weren't for the cover of darkness.

"Oh, God, Jules," he says, and it sounds like he's about to break down again. "I miss you like you have no idea. I know I sound like a basket case, and I'm sorry for—jeez, for slobbering all over—but this has been the longest week, and everything's so . . . fucked up. . . ."

"Yeah."

"I need to tell you about it. There's stuff I haven't told you."

I nod. "I want to hear it all. I want to help you. I will be there, helping you. Okay? I mean, do you know when it's going to happen? Probably not . . ."

"No idea."

I close my eyes, feeling defeat. "We'll get it. I just need to figure out how to get out of here. I'm suffocating."

"We both are."

We're quiet for a minute.

"Stay on the phone with me," he says. "Please?"

"I will." I climb back into bed and pull the blankets over me, keeping the phone to my ear. "I've never slept with a boy before," I say.

He laughs a little and it makes me feel better for him. We whisper a little bit, and soon we're quiet. My eyelids droop.

In an instant, it's morning.

Nine

"What happened to your face?" Rowan asks as we stand in the bathroom together, putting finishing touches on our makeup.

I glare. "Nothing." The imprint of the cell phone remains on my cheek, though it's not nearly as pronounced as when I first got up.

She narrows her eyes at me, suspicious. "You know," she says, "I don't mind picking up shifts for you in case you're, like, feeling a little *overtired*. Or if you need to go to the *library* for a *project* or something. I like money."

I pause and look at her in the mirror.

"Or maybe you want to, I don't know, *volunteer* somewhere on Saturday mornings."

I set my can of hair spray down. "Hmm."

"You need to get a little creative is all I'm saying. Don't you want to join a club after school? Try out for a sport?" She blinks her lashes rapidly and smiles.

I snort. "Yeah," I say, waving my cast. "Sports."

"Well, I'm just trying to help." She puts away her makeup and glances at one of the seventeen clocks—the top one, which actually works—that the hoarder decided would look great piled on the towel rack above the toilet. "Let's go."

I nod. "Thanks."

As we grab our coats and backpacks, I ask her, "What do you do with all your money, anyway?"

"Save it."

"For what?"

"My trip to New York. Spring break. I'm going to see Charlie." She patters down the stairs.

My jaw drops, and I follow her. "You're what?"

She shrugs. "I already have my plane ticket."

"You—you—" I sputter. We climb into the running car, where Trey is waiting, tapping the steering wheel with an annoyed look on his face. "Mom and Dad are letting you go? I can't believe it."

"Letting her go where?" Trey asks. He takes off quickly down the alley and turns onto the street.

Rowan is quiet from the backseat. I turn and look at her, and she's pressing her lips together.

"Oh my dog," I say. "You haven't told them?"

"Told them what?" Trey asks.

"Well," Rowan says, "since I have you both here, I'm going to need some help covering my shifts. You both owe me plenty."

"What's going on?" Trey says in an outdoor voice.

I stare at Rowan. "Do you have any scope of realization of what you are about to unleash upon us all? They'll call the freaking cops! Report you as a missing person!"

Trey pulls the car over on the side of the road. "What. Is. Happening!" he shouts, eyes ablaze.

I turn my attention to Trey. "Rowan has a boyfriend in New York and she's going to see him over spring break."

Trey whirls around, eyes bulging. "What?"

Rowan's gaze settles somewhere to the left of and below Trey's jaw. She starts biting her lip. "I'm going," she says weakly.

"You're fifteen!" he says. "Mom is going to blow a freaking gasket. Who is this loser?"

Rowan gets her courage back. "He's not a loser! He's— his name is Charlie."

"Charles something something Banks," I interject.

"The third," Rowan adds, which is news to me. "His parents invited me. They paid for my ticket, but I already told them I'll pay them back when I get there." She adjusts her collar. "We met at soccer camp."

"He has a live-in tutor," I offer.

"Not live-in," Rowan says.

"She's met his parents."

Trey blinks. And then he shakes his head. "You little creep," he mutters, checking his mirrors and pulling back onto the road. "Why can't *I* ever find a Charles something something the third?"

I face forward. "So you're okay with this?" I ask him.

He gives a bitter laugh. "Fuck," he says. "Why the hell not." He punches the gas a little harder than usual and pulls into the school parking lot. "Why the hell not," he says again. He parks a few rows from Sawyer's car and looks over his shoulder at Rowan as he turns off the car and pulls out the keys. "You're going to be the one who actually survives this family, aren't you. The only one."

Rowan just stares at him, and then he's out and slamming the door, shoulders curved and head bowed to the wind.

We get out. "What was that all about?" she asks as Sawyer gets out of his car, sees me, and heads toward us.

I shrug, but I think I know, because I used to feel it too. Trey's jealous. "I think maybe he wishes he had something you have," I say. But I don't take the time to explain, because Sawyer is standing on my shadow and his ropy lashes are about to lasso me in.

Gag. That was bad.

Ten

Rowan melts into the sea of students and Sawyer is pulling me to the side of the school building. "When," he says.

"What?"

"When can I see you? I need to see you. After school? Say yes. Say yes. Say yes."

"I—" I begin, and the rest of the automatic sentence, *have to work*, drops away. His cheeks are flushed with the cold. "Okay," I say.

"Okay?" He sounds shocked.

"Yes," I say, grabbing some of Rowan's boldness before it dissipates. "I—I'll join a group. Volunteer."

"What?"

"Nothing. Alibi. Just thinking out loud. Don't you have to work?"

"I switched with Kate."

Kate. The cousin in college. Kate with the funky blond hair whose life I saved. "Right. Excellent. Rowan will cover for me. Okay." I take a breath and decide specifically not to think about what my father will do to me when I don't come home. Trey will help. As we walk into school together I start reading posted signs on the walls for the first time in my high school career. "Pep Club? No, no way. Too much Roxie and BFF Sarah. Psych Club . . . a-ha-ha-ha, no comment." I keep looking. And then I turn to see Sawyer watching me, that little smile on his lips. "Do you play chess?" I ask.

"Um, why? Is this a trick question to determine if I'm too awesome for you?"

"No no no, I'm just looking for a club to join so I have an excuse to see you. I could tell my parents I'm in a chess club, but then I might have to, you know, eventually, um, prove that I know how to play."

He's still smiling at me. My brain turns to fuzz.

"Yes," he says. "I play chess." We stop at my locker and he says, "In fact, I was thinking about starting an exclusive chess club for offspring of pizza proprietors."

I grin. "Oh my dogs, I believe I qualify."

"We'll have a lot of meetings," he warns.

"I'll be there—as often as I can." I ignore the nervous quake in my gut that taunts, *Your parents will find out.*

His face is close to mine. "Tonight's launch meeting is from three to five thirty. I'll have you back at the restaurant by then. Will that work okay?"

I nod. Whisper, "We'll get this vision thing figured out, Sawyer. I promise."

The bell rings. Sawyer's smile turns reluctant and he caresses my neck, one slick motion that makes my hip sockets burst into flames.

Trey promises to tell Mom that I joined a chess club (dotcom, he says wickedly, so I have to kick him), and that I'll be home by five thirty. And that I would have called her myself but I still don't have a cell phone. Not one she knows of, anyway.

I load up my backpack more slowly than usual, letting the halls clear around me. Sawyer saunters up to me and we walk down the hallway together. Ever so casually he takes my hand, entwining his fingers with mine. And then my eyes get all misty. Stupid, I know, but you know what? I remember thinking there would never be a time when I'd hold a boy's hand in the hallway at school, much less the love of my life's. It's all a little emotional there for a second, because here I am, and it feels even better than it looks. I squeeze his hand

and he squeezes back and looks sidelong at me, and I am so in love.

He opens the car door for me, which feels so incredibly awkward that I hurriedly ask him not to do that again, unless I'm, like, carrying a six-foot sheet cake or something. And then we set out for somewhere, I'm not sure where. He takes my hand again and puts it on the stick shift with his. When he pushes in the clutch I change gears for him, and we're flying out of town, away from Melrose Park, away from people who frown at us for stupid reasons. After a few minutes Sawyer pulls into a community college parking lot and parks by the gymnasium. Without a word we get out and he pulls me through the snow to the side of the building. There are a few cubbyholes in the wall and I can hear fans running. I catch a whiff of chlorine and feel a blast of humid air on my cheeks.

Sawyer and I duck inside one of the indents and suddenly it's warm. "Pool fan," he says, facing me. "My brothers told me about this trick."

I stare at him. We are alone.

At last, at last.

I lunge for his coat, unbuttoning it, and I slide my hands to his neck, pull his head toward mine, trying not to scrape him with my clunky cast. His hands suspend in the air for a second, and then he buries them in my hair and we're kissing and panting and touching each other, starving and lusty and steamy hot, and soon he's wrenching my coat off and pulling off his own, and he presses against me, his chest against my chest, our feet finding spaces every other, and his thighs squeezing mine. And suddenly I realize that what's pressing against me is not all thigh, and I am secretly amazed and a little shocked by it being there, doing that. He moans and drags his lips to my neck, and my hands flounder at his hips and slide over them into his back pockets, like my fingers are someone else's expert sexy fingers and I'm the lucky one who gets to feel through them, because dog knows I don't know what I'm doing, I'm just going with it, intoxicated by his fervor and the overwhelming electric, psychedelic aching in my loins.

"Oh my God," he whispers after a few minutes, breathing hard, and he lifts heavy hands one by one and slaps them against the wall behind me, pushing away, forcing space between us. He leans forward, arching his back, and rests his forehead on my shoulder, panting. "Shit. You are dangerous."

I pet the back of his head, my lips tingling. "Are you okay?"

He lifts his head and looks at me, and it's a look I don't recognize. Desire and heat and I don't know what else. "My God," he says again, shaking his head a little. "What the heck was I thinking all those years?" He mops his face with a hand and looks at the coats on the cement pad at our feet. "I mean, it's—" He looks around, distracted, like he forgot where we are. "It's not just the *this* stuff, but the *this* is . . . probably . . ." He nods to himself. "Yeah. It's going to kill me. For sure."

I am intrigued by his random candidness, and I think how funny it is that I can make ball jokes until I'm blue in the face (dot-com) but I'm sooo inexperienced in the actual *this* of things, that I'm not quite sure what should or should not be happening on what I'm starting to think of as our first date. Which is also *my* first date ever. I'm pretty sure coats on the ground is far enough, though.

I reach up and kiss him again, lightly this time, and then turn my head and rest it on his shoulder, holding him. But those last words from him ring in my ears. *Yeah. It's going to kill me. For sure.* And that reminds me of something else entirely unsexy, which makes my stomach clutch. I glance at my phone to check the time, and my brain totally changes gears. "Sit with me," I say. I slide down the wall and sit, enveloped in the warmth from the swimming pool circulation fan. He hesitates and eases down to sit too. And then, together, we sigh. The fun is over, and we turn our attention to the urgent matter of the vision that is taking over Sawyer's life.

Eleven

He pulls out a folded wad of paper from his pants pocket and opens it. The late-afternoon sun glows orange through nearby branches as he looks at his notes.

"First of all, this sucks," he says. "Making out was way more fun."

"Making out is my favorite," I say glumly.

"Right?" He folds the papers with one hand and puts his other to his forehead, rubbing his temples. "Okay, so here's how it goes."

I link my arm in his and scoot my butt closer.

"We're in a classroom. You asked me how I knew before, and I couldn't tell you back then, but now I know. In a couple of the frames, as my view—or whatever—pans the room, there's a whiteboard on the wall and a few tables and overturned chairs."

"I always thought of my view as the camera angle," I say. "You see what the camera sees, right? And the angle changes a few times? Mine did, anyway."

He nods. "Yeah, it does. That's totally how it looks." He rests his hand on mine, absently traces my fingers. "So the first scene, I guess, is from a back corner of the classroom. The camera does a fast pan of the room and lands on a person—the gunman. He's wearing dark-wash jeans and a black fleece jacket, and he's got a floppy knit cap on his head." He turns toward me a fraction. "Any questions so far?"

"Yeah," I say. "About a hundred. Was there a clock or calendar anywhere?"

"Not that I saw."

"Any writing on the whiteboard?"

"Yes, but I couldn't read it."

"A lot?"

"A few lines."

"Like math equations or like sentences?"

"Sentences. Outline form. Ish."

I rummage around in my coat pockets for a pen. I always used to keep a few handy for when I was doing deliveries. I find one in an interior pocket and pull it out. Sawyer hands me the notes, and I start jotting down things on the back of one page. "Okay, so probably not a math class, right?"

"Hunh. I guess that's a reasonable assumption."

"Did the guy have any snow on his shoulders or hat?"

"Um, I didn't notice. I don't think so."

I start a second list on a different sheet of paper—things for Sawyer to look for next time.

"Did you get any view of the windows?"

He squeezes his eyes shut, thinking. "You know, I think maybe I did, but I don't remember anything about them. The windows felt . . . dark. I'll look again."

I write that down and ask, "How tall was the guy?"

"Kind of short."

"How could you tell?"

He pauses. "In relation to the tables, he seemed short. Thin build."

I nod. "Boots or shoes?"

His mouth parts and then closes again, and I write that one down for him to check on.

"It was dark, you said the other day. Darkish, anyway, because you could see the muzzle whatever fire thingy."

"Yeah. Not totally dark. More like . . . dimly lit."

"So it could just be from the shades being drawn? Like they were doing something with a projector? Or maybe it was stormy outside?"

"Maybe. I don't know." He sets his jaw. "I don't know."

"I'm sorry."

"No, it's okay. You're asking great questions. It's just . . . hard."

I nod. After a minute I ask, "What about the next scene?"

He looks at his notes. "Okay, so the angle changes. The camera, I mean. I think it's at the front of the room, because the wall I can see in this next scene doesn't have a whiteboard and the tables are on the left instead of the right. I—"

"Wait. Is anybody sitting at the tables or are the chairs empty?"

"Empty. Disorderly. Some of the chairs are tipped over."

"There are no people? Just the shooter?" I watch his face. He stares straight ahead.

"There . . . are people." His eyes glaze.

A shiver rolls down my back. Finally I whisper, "Where are the people, Sawyer?"

"They're . . . in the back corner."

"They're standing in the back corner of the room?"

"Not standing." His voice is wispy under the grumble of the fan. His eyelids droop shut and his face grows pained. "They're . . . they're on the floor. And there's . . . stuff . . . everywhere."

My stomach turns, and I don't want to ask. "Stuff?"

He nods. "I don't want to tell you."

I can barely breathe. "You mean blood."

"Yes. Blood."

"More than blood?"

He takes in a sudden breath and blows it out through his mouth. "Yeah. Guts and brains, I guess. And . . . that's all."

I pull my hand out from under his and rub my forehead, almost feeling sick. I know how real the vision must look to him. And I know he's looking at me to say something that can give him some hope. But it's a long reach. "The thing is," I say in a quiet voice, "is that if we get this right, and we find this classroom, and we stop this gunman, that scene will go away. It won't happen. They won't get shot, and they won't die. Right?"

He's frozen.

"Right," I answer for him. "So we focus on finding the date, time, and place. And we don't focus on the bodies and the blood and the . . . the stuff."

This time he nods, and after a minute he looks at me. "The only time I think there's any chance at all to save them is when you're with me."

I give him a grim smile. "Oh, there's definitely a chance." I think about it for a minute—the vision police, or the president of scenes, whoever or whatever controls this beastly mind game—and I say, "I don't think we'd get this chance to save people if it was hopeless."

As I say it, I try to convince myself that I believe it.

Twelve

Five things that you can never truly understand
unless you live through them:
1. Hoarding
2. Visions of dead people
3. Driving a giant meatball truck to school
4. Depression
5. Love
6. Sexy time

Okay, so that was six, but I could probably come up
with even more. Shall I elaborate on said list? I say no on
numbers one through four.

Number five—I just really had no idea how painful
love is. I mean, my love is different for Sawyer than for

anybody else I love. If Trey was the one going through this vision thing, I think I could handle it better. Oh, it aches, the love. Gah. I hate my pathetic overdramatic self.

Number six. Sexy time—I guess I'm trying to process this one. Let's just say that weird things happen when you get all sexy with somebody. I seriously didn't understand this even from reading some of the skanky books my dad brings home from yard sales that Mom forbids us to read. Like, during sexy time, stuff happens physically and mentally and emotionally *all at the same time*, and you kind of lose your mind a little bit. Let's dissect.

First, you're just minding your own business one day when something inside you randomly decides that you are attracted to a certain person, and you really have no control over it. Like, one day he's just some guy in your math class, or some boy you played plastic cheetahs and bears with in first grade. And then before you know it, he's like a freaking sex magnet and you can't stop thinking about him. What the heck? He says something or does something that changes absolutely everything. You used to think he had a big nose, but now it's perfect or whatever. Or you thought you'd never like a person with zits, but then you totally change your mind and decide zits aren't so bad after all. And if you kind of look at them in a different, intense way—and I seriously did not factor in the power of all the possible ways to look at someone—it makes your body get all electric and wilty inside, and so you decide, hey, I wanna suck face with that person. What?

Seriously? I mean, I care about germs. I do. I work in a restaurant, and we have rules upon rules, and I am a stoic follower of germ rules. But if Sawyer Angotti wants to put his germy tongue (GERMY TONGUE NOT RELATED TO HAIRY TONGUE) in my mouth, I will welcome it. What has happened here?

Yeah, I took health class–slash–sex ed, and I learned all that textbook stuff, like that the first sign of pregnancy is missing your period and that whole "point of no return" and shit like that. But they do not, I repeat, they do not teach you about that delicious, delirious, buttery, melty feeling between your legs.

I'm not trying to be gross or weird here. I'm just saying there is no teaching or describing this in any possibly accurate way. Parents do not tell their children about this, even the hippie parents who are all like "sex is beautiful" and stuff. There is only discovering it when you are going through that whole rationalization scene—how you used to think other people's tongues were disgusting, and then suddenly in *one instant* they're, like, the best thing ever and you want it in your mouth, like, *now*.

And let's talk about the boys. And how things like penises are so weird and awkward and probably superugly, and then they, like, *react* to things like they are alive and living their own little life in your pants—I don't know. Like a freaking barnacle or something. And as a girl, I'm sorry, but I have never really thought about this penis factor as it pertains to me. And boys? I have to say that I am very sympathetic. Because what if, like, my boobs or my elbow or something totally wigged out into the shape of the Eiffel Tower whenever I started kissing someone I liked? I mean, seriously. How embarrassing. But guess what? Because of number six, suddenly it's not embarrassing, because we're in some sort of bizarre temporary world where such things are acceptable.

And I'm not talking about *actual* sex, okay. I mean, I just had my first kiss, so it's not like I'm experienced enough to address that. I'm talking about the attraction thing and the mushy gut stuff that goes with that.

And it's those feelings that I am most shocked by. Indescribable. Which means, of course, I want like hell to describe it.

I think I might even write my next psych paper about it. Poor Mr. Polselli.

But the last thing I need to say about this is that I should not, not, not be thinking about sexy time when Sawyer is having a vision portraying a freaking homicidal maniac who blows people's brains out. I mean, how awful am I that my mind and my dreams return to sexy time again and again? Pretty freaking awful.

But here's the thing that's even worse. What if Sawyer can't save those people, and he dies trying? Seriously, what if he dies? I don't know if I can handle it. After all I did to save him with my vision, I have to go through this all over again, only somehow, now that we are together, it's a hundred times worse. Because I'm the one with a crazy, endlessly depressed father and these crazy psycho genes, and I infected Sawyer with this vision that he has no choice but to obey.

If he dies? It'll feel like I killed him myself.

Thirteen

"Chess club," my dad says from the single uncluttered chair in the darkened living room. The blue haze from the muted TV hangs low in the room, making his hoards of junk look even weightier somehow.

Tonight I did my first shift of deliveries since the crash. Somebody had a late-night craving that we agreed to satisfy even though technically the restaurant was closed. By the time I got back the place was dark.

I take off my coat. "Yeah," I say.

"They start a new club in the middle of the second semester?"

My left eye starts to twitch. "No, it's been going on all year." I hang my coat up and start down the hallway.

"Come back here," he says.

I stop in my tracks and turn around slowly and walk to the doorway of the living room. "It's late, Dad," I say. "I'm exhausted."

"Chess club will do that to you." He's not looking at me.

My stomach is clenched. But I'm mad too. "No, actually, working a six-hour shift after chess club on a school night will do that to me."

"You don't know how to play chess." It's a challenge.

"That's why I wanted to learn," I lie, and I'm surprised how easy it is to lie to someone you've lost all respect for. "I was thinking about trying out for a sport, but with the cast, my options are limited."

"Is that Angotti boy in chess club?" He turns to look at me for the first time. He hasn't shaved in a few days.

I meet his gaze. It would be so easy to just tell the truth and say no. Instead, my big mouth shows up. "Why don't you call his parents to find out?"

His eyes flare and he squeezes the arms of the chair. He looks like he's going to ream me out, but he holds it in.

After a moment I force a smile. "Night," I say, and turn around, heading back down the hallway to my room. Once inside I let out the breath of fear I'd been holding. Note to self: Learn how to play chess. Now.

"I need to learn how to play chess," I say when I see Sawyer the next morning.

"Yes, yes you do."

"Like, for real."

He nods seriously. And then he narrows his eyes. "Wait. You mean literally."

I grin. "Yes, you horn dog. My dad's suspicious."

"Oh. Well, then." He contemplates this as we walk in the direction of our first-hour classes. And then he stops outside his classroom and his face brightens. "No problem. We'll do it at lunch. I just remembered—there happens to be an app for this situation."

I laugh. "Wouldn't it be cool if there was an app for figuratively playing chess?"

His green eyes bore holes in mine. "No. I only like the real thing." He pulls my hand toward his mouth, never taking his eyes off mine, and lets his lips linger on my thumb knuckle. Then he gives me that shy grin and disappears into his classroom.

Big sigh, Demarco.

At lunch Sawyer downloads a chess app on his phone and starts explaining the game pieces and what they do. Trey looks on, mildly interested. After a while he says, "Maybe I should join chess club."

Sawyer and I look at him.

He frowns. "Not your euphemistic club. Duh. I'm not into incest, thank you. However . . ." He raises an eyebrow at Sawyer. "If you ever, you know, want to experiment . . ."

I punch Trey in the arm.

Sawyer grins. "Maybe I could bang all the Demarco siblings."

"Ack! This conversation is so inappropriate," I say, and I feel my face getting hot. "Now I can't get that image out of my head, you losers. Don't drag poor, innocent Rowan into this love triangle, please."

Trey pipes up. "It would be a quadrangle—a love rhombus. Not pretty. And two equal teams would end up in a draw. But at least two of the Demarcos would be—"

"Stop," I say, putting my hands over my ears, and they stop, finally. Guys are so weird and gross. But it's good to see Sawyer having a little fun in the middle of this mess.

Sawyer's fun doesn't last long. After school he's waiting for me outside with a serious look on his face. I glance at Trey and Rowan, who stop with me. "You guys go ahead," I say to them. "Tell Mom I had to go to the library." I turn to Sawyer. "Can you drop me off later?"

"Yeah, of course."

"Cool." I turn back to Trey. "I'll be home before five. We just need to talk about . . . some stuff."

Trey and Rowan glance at each other and then back at me. "Okay," Trey says. He shrugs and they get in the delivery car.

When they leave, I look at Sawyer. "What happened?"

"Had a film in biology today."

"And?"

"Supposedly it was about amphibians."

I wait.

"All I saw was twenty minutes' worth of the vision on constant repeat. Gunshots in my head every four seconds." He taps out the rhythm on the car door.

"Sorry." I cringe, thinking of the gory mess he described. "Did you see anything else?"

"Yeah. There's new stuff."

"Helpful?"

He shrugs. "I don't know. It's so quick. But then something else happened."

I narrow my eyes. "What?"

"After the film was done, we opened our textbooks, and all I could see was the vision." He brings a gloved hand to his eyes and shakes his head a little. "I think I'm losing it, Jules. I'm not sure I can handle this. Not sure at all."

Fourteen

We go to the library and sit at the computers. I tell Sawyer to pull up a video while I take some notebook paper and a pencil out of my backpack.

"Are you seeing it?"

"One sec," he says, pushing play. "Yeah." He presses pause, rewinds, and hits play, then pause again.

"Okay. What do you see?"

"Hey—can't I just print—"

"Ah, no. Tried that. Doesn't work."

He frowns. "This is one of the new pieces. It's our guy walking. He's outside, wearing the same clothes."

"Bonus. Finally. Is it dark or light out?"

"Dusk."

"What do you see?"

"A sidewalk. Grass. A bare tree."

"Grass?"

He nods. "Brownish-yellow grass, all flat and wet."

"Any buds on that tree?"

"No. Eh . . . wait. Yes, tiny buds. It's blurry."

"Any snow at all?"

"No, just wet grass and wet sidewalk."

I look out the library window. There's snow on the ground a couple of inches deep, but huge honking piles of the dirty kind along the road and the sidewalk. On my computer I check the weather report. The ten-day forecast shows a quick warming trend with rain on the weekend and temperatures reaching the sixties by next Tuesday. One week from today.

"Shit," I mutter. "Rain plus warmth equals snow melted by this weekend." I look at Sawyer. "How bad has the vision been, exactly?"

Sawyer stares at the computer. His hand shakes on the mouse. "Bad. It's everywhere."

"Car windows?"

"Sometimes."

"Mirrors too?"

"Yes."

I stare at him. "Why didn't you tell me?"

"I—I thought I was telling you."

"Well, yeah, but you didn't say it was getting so

intense. That means it's happening soon!" My whisper is on the verge of breaking decibel records.

He turns to me, his eyes weary and red rimmed. "I know. But there's no fucking information here, okay? I can't *do* anything unless it tells me how to find it!"

"Sawyer, there *has* to be something there. That's the way it works! You have to look for stuff!"

"That's the way it worked for you," he says, no longer whispering. He pushes his chair back. "You keep telling me I'm doing it wrong, but you don't see it. You don't know. There are no body bags, no faces I can recognize, because the faces are all blown to bits. Okay? There's nothing there that I recognize. You had a building that you could figure out. You had a face you recognized, and that helped you put it all together. Me? I don't have jack shit."

I stare at him. He stares back. And I think about what I just said and close my eyes. "God, you're right," I say finally. "I'm sorry, Sawyer, I don't know what I'm saying."

The intensity on his face wanes a little, but he leans forward and adds, "Don't treat me like I'm stupid just because my vision is different from yours. I get what we're trying to do here. I'm doing my best."

I hang my head. Dear dogs. What am I doing to him? Nothing like adding another layer of pressure—as if the vision wasn't enough. "Sorry," I say again.

He gives me a rueful smile. "S'okay. I know you're worried too. You must feel pretty helpless."

I nod. "Anyway," I say.

"Anyway," he agrees. "Okay, so I liked the questions you were asking earlier. That was helpful."

I nod again. And I like that we just talked this out. No big fight, nobody getting all hurt feelings or acting passive-aggressive or whatever . . . it's nice. As nice as it can be, anyway. "In this frame, are there any buildings?"

"No. But there's a road. More like, um, not a public road with painted lines or anything—it's like a private paved road."

"Like a school would have. Makes sense. Any signs? Street signs, big cement block signs, school marquee-type signs in the distance?"

"There's a little stop sign down at the end of the road. Not like full size."

"Can you see the sky?"

"The sky? Yeah, I guess. It's dark, cloudy."

"No sign of a sun or sunset or anything?"

"No."

I take a few notes. "Any idea what kind of tree that is?"

He squints. "It's got really thin branches. The trunk is sort of squat and rounded and the branches are like long, narrow fingers going everywhere."

I frown. "Like a weeping willow? All hanging down like hair?"

"No, more like . . . hmm. Like the kinds of trees that line downtown streets, you know? They aren't like hulking oaks or maples; they're daintier, low to the ground, like a big bush."

"A flowering tree, maybe?" I tilt my head, trying to picture it. "Here, can you draw?"

"Not well." But he takes the pencil and tries.

"What if you hold up the paper to the monitor and trace it?"

He glances sidelong at me. "Smart." He does it, and it's so weird to see him tracing something I can't see. The bare branches look like fish skeletons. "I don't know what good this will do."

"I know. Probably none. But at least we're accomplishing something. How's the vision now—if you look out the window, is it there?"

He turns his head and looks. "No, not at the moment."

I smile. "Good."

"So we're doing something right?"

"I think so."

"About time."

We go through the vision frame by frame until it's almost five and I have to go. Sawyer drops me off a block from the restaurant. "Thanks," he says. "It's nice talking things through, you know? My family always just yells."

"It was really nice. Sorry I was in your face."

He leans over and we kiss, slow and sweet, and then I get out and head to work, wondering if Depressed Dad is oblivious to my nonappearance or if Angry Dad will be waiting by the back door for me.

Fifteen

Lucky for me, no one notices me slipping in because my parents are too busy admiring the shiny new ball truck in the back parking lot. I dump my coat and backpack, throw on an apron, and go out back to join them in the cold. The giant meatballs are the same, but the lettering and logo on the side of the truck are fresh and bold. Inside it's pretty much brand-new, customized to Dad's requests, with all-new cooking equipment and fixtures and extra storage from what we were used to. It's actually pretty nice, as food trucks go. Here's hoping it puts Dad in a better mood.

"I hear it's warming up this weekend," I say, trying to pretend I've been here all along. "Can't wait to try it out. There's a food truck festival in the city. Heard about it on Twitter."

Trey snorts and gives me a look.

I grin and shrug, rubbing my arms to keep warm. My cast snags my sweater, not for the first time. Annoying. I frown and poke the yarn into the new hole with my pinkie. "I'm going inside to see if Aunt Mary needs help," I say.

"Me too," Rowan says.

We run in together.

"Is Dad pissed?" I ask.

"No, he didn't say anything. Giant balls saved the day," Rowan says. We clear the snow from our boots.

"Sorry to put you guys in an awkward position again."

"Don't worry," Rowan says, hanging up her coat. She looks over her shoulder at me and fluffs her hair before she puts it up into her usual work ponytail. "I'll get you back."

The first customers are arriving as we check in with Aunt Mary, and my mind strays to Sawyer and the new scenes. It's frustrating, not being able to see the vision. I feel like I'm removed from it in a big way. Like it isn't really happening because I can't see it, and this is just a puzzle I need to solve. Like eleven gunshots are just ricocheting in some movie I haven't been to.

But it's real. It'll happen to real people, and to their real families, whether we're there or not. It's the kind of horrendous tragedy that makes national headlines. And somehow, in my mind, a guy with a gun that could go off in any direction and end lives in an instant seems so much more random and dangerous than a single snowplow hitting a single building. Like the snowplow is easier to control than one person's arm.

Around nine we have a lull, so Mom and I are starting cleanup in the kitchen. When I feel my phone vibrating under my apron, I grab the bags of trash and run them out to the Dumpster.

"Hey," I say. "I have about ten seconds."

"Okay. Something wasn't sitting right, so I went back to the library after I dropped you off. I watched the vision again, then rewound all the way and realized there's a single frame so quick I missed it—it was just a little flash right after the short scene with the grass and sidewalk. And it took me forever to land on it just right, but finally I did, and there's a building."

I suck in a breath. "Okay?"

"It's an old building with ivy on it. I can only see part of it. I sketched it. I'll bring it tomorrow."

"'Kay. Gotta run. Good job." I slide the phone into my pocket again as Trey pulls up after finishing deliveries. I toss the trash into the Dumpster with my good arm and meet Trey on the way to the door.

"Slow night," he says. "Nothing new come in?"

"Nada. You get to help us clean up." I grin.

Before we go inside he pauses, his hand on the knob, and turns to look at me. "Is there something going on with you and Sawyer besides . . . you know. The usual kisskiss stuff?"

I try to stop my eyes from darting around guiltily, but I've never been good at lying to Trey. "Well, I'm not pregnant, if that's what you're wondering. Again. Be sure and tell Dad and everyone."

He laughs. "No, I wasn't thinking that. Sawyer just looks . . ."

"Hot?"

"No. Well, yeah, but—"

"Sexay?"

He sighs. "Stressed out."

I just press my lips together in a grim smile and shrug.

After a minute, Trey nods. "Okay." He starts up the steps to the restaurant and turns. "Well, if you ever need an ear." I can tell he's trying not to look hurt.

"Thanks, big brother," I say, and reach out to squeeze his arm.

He messes up my hair. "Dork," he says. He turns the handle and we go inside.

At night, when I lie in bed staring at the ceiling and watching the blinking lights from the sign outside, I think about what schools might be composed of old-looking buildings with ivy on them. The last thought I have as I drift off: *Probably in the city.*

Sixteen

In the morning I'm on the computer early, researching Chicago's oldest school buildings still in use. I scribble notes to myself—"Lincoln Park. Old Chicago. Survived the big fire? Grass. Bushy trees. Private road. Small stop sign."

Not all of the older schools I can find have pictures online, and besides, our stinking slow connection makes it impossibly hard for me to load anything, so I give up on that and start to list school names on a different paper. "Drive by: Lincoln Park HS. Lake View HS. Wendell Phillips Academy. Robert Lindblom Math/Science Acad."

And then I add questions.

1. Victims are presumably high school age, not
   middle school, right? Can tell by clothes/

dress/size? Maturity—boobs/facial hair?
Note clothing of each victim—for identifying before.
2. Close-up of whiteboard—forgot to tell you
about zooming the pic to read the writing.
3. . . .

It's right about here that I realized these notes could be vastly misunderstood, maybe even peg me as plotting a school shooting if they end up in the wrong hands, and I nearly choke at the thought. What a kick in the teeth. I debate ripping this up and swallowing it vs. burning it, and then decide I'm being irrational and just fold it up and put it in my pocket.

In the five seconds that remain before Rowan drags me out the door, I leave a note on the kitchen counter by the sink. "Going to library after school for tree research. Our lame Internet connection is too slow—can't get my homework done."

"Tree research?" Rowan asks as we three climb into the car.

"Yeah. It's for a . . . project."

Trey turns his head sharply to stare at me. "I don't remember having to do any tree project in tenth grade," he says. He looks back at the road, but I can feel an accusation in his posture.

I shrug. "Maybe it's new." My hands start to sweat.

"Look," he says, glancing in the rearview mirror, "I know something's up. You're a terrible liar. And you're starting to piss me off."

I sigh. "Nothing's up. Not with me. Okay? Sawyer needs my help on something."

Tension strains the silence.

"It's not my thing to tell," I say.

After a few quiet minutes, we're at school and Trey parks the car. We all climb out.

"Go ahead, Ro," he says.

She rolls her eyes. "You'd better include me this time if it's something exciting and dangerous, that's all I can say." She shrugs her backpack strap higher on her shoulder and walks toward the school.

Trey comes around the front of the car and stops me, a shock of his sleek dark waves falling over one eye. "After all I did for you, *and* for him, I think I deserve to know what's going on. Or you can forget about me covering for you like this day after day. Okay? I'm done."

He stares at me for a long moment, black eyes piercing into mine, and then he turns on the wet pavement and strides through the parking lot, leaving me standing there looking at the rivulets of water migrating from the shrinking piles of crusty, dirty snow.

• • •

Inside, Sawyer hands me a folded piece of paper, and I hand him one in return. We both open them and read them, standing together at my locker. I skim his long, detailed outline, my eyes growing wider as I read. When I get to the bottom, I look at him. "Seriously?"

He nods, staring blankly at the paper I gave him, and then he looks at me. "There's no way we can do this alone," he says in a low voice.

"I've been thinking about that. What about . . . Trey?" I ask.

He nods again. "I don't know who else to go to." His voice is hollow, and his hand drops to his side like he's too tired to hold the paper any longer.

"No, this is good," I say. "Really. He already knows something's up." I fold the notes he gave me into a tight square and put them safely in my pocket. "I'll talk to him and see if we can figure out a time to meet up so we can explain—"

Just then Roxie and BFF Sarah come up behind Sawyer. Roxie slaps Sawyer on the butt, and when he turns, Sarah grabs the paper from his hand.

"Ooh, a love note!" She laughs.

Sawyer tries to grab it but Sarah hands it off to Roxie. And because of my paranoia this morning, and because it's so stupid rude anyway, I lunge for the paper, grasp Roxie's shirt collar with my good hand, and pull the paper from her with my other hand, leaving only a tiny bit between her fingers and, unfortunately, a large scratch on her neck from my fingernail.

"Ow, you bitch!" she shrieks, holding her neck like it's way more than just a flesh wound, and then she lunges back at me, going for my neck rather than the paper, which I manage to shove into my pocket.

People around us start shouting and I can't see anything but Roxie's flaring nostrils in my face. I think frantically about how this all will lead to nothing good, namely parents being called, and I sink to the floor, deadweight, praying that somebody pulls her off me as she follows me to the floor, because I'm not going to fight back. In an instant, she digs her knee into my stomach and rakes her fake claws down my neck. I close my eyes and keep my flinching as invisible as possible, hoping she doesn't totally fuck up my innards after they've been trying so hard to heal. Instinctively I bring my good arm up to her rib cage to try to lessen the weight she's putting on me, and she jabs her elbow into my biceps, giving me a wicked charley horse.

"Stop!" I hear, and realize it's my hoarse voice yelling.

The whole thing lasts about five seconds, maybe a few more than that, but it feels like an hour before her knee is off my gut. I'm not quite flat on the floor; my head is against the lockers and my neck is twisted. I open an eye as Sawyer kneels down to see if I'm okay and help me up, and I look at Roxie, who is being held back by the guy whose locker is next to mine. Mr. Polselli stands between us, his hand on Roxie's shoulder, his eyes on me.

"Are you okay?" Sawyer asks.

I nod quickly and scramble to get to my feet, embarrassed. We're surrounded by students eager for a girl fight. "Sorry to disappoint," I say to them, catching my breath. I hold my cast in front of me and my good arm pressed against my stomach and make a pained face. Hey, I'm not stupid.

"My classroom," Mr. Polselli barks at both of us just as the bell rings. "Everybody else get out of here."

Sawyer tries to come with me, but Mr. Polselli gives him the hairy eyeball. Sawyer says how sorry he is with his eyes, and then he frowns and grabs his books, watching at least until we're out of sight and inside the psych classroom. Mr. Polselli's papier-mâché bust of Ivan Pavlov stares at me.

"Roxanne, you start," Mr. Polselli says.

"She attacked me and cut my neck," Roxie says. "I can feel it. See?"

"Why did she attack you?"

"Because she's a paranoid freak," she says. "She can't stand that I'm friends with her boyfriend."

"I did not *attack* you. You *took*—" I begin, but Mr. Polselli holds a hand up to me. Students start to come into the room, and they send curious looks in our direction.

"So she scratched you, and you scratched her back four times. And pushed her to the ground?"

"No, she fell." Roxie won't look at me, but her eyes are brimming, and I feel strangely sorry for her for the briefest moment.

Mr. Polselli turns to me. "Julia, did you attack Roxanne?"

"No, I was reaching for something and I accidentally scratched her. I wasn't trying to do that."

"What were you reaching for?"

"A note. Her friend Sarah pulled it from Sawyer Angotti's hand and gave it to her. They think it's a love note. It was something private I gave him, and she was just, I don't know, goofing around or whatever, and I reacted, trying to get it back." I pause, setting my jaw so I don't cry. I have never been in trouble like this before. "I'm sorry I scratched you, Rox. I didn't mean to. I just wanted the paper back." My fingers go to my own neck, which throbs now, and I wonder how bad my scratches are. I can feel the raised welts.

My biggest fear is that Mr. Polselli asks to see the paper, but I'm prepared to say no—it's not like we got caught in class passing notes or something. School hadn't even started yet. But he doesn't ask for it, and I breathe a silent sigh of relief.

"Roxanne?" Mr. Polselli asks. "Do you have anything else to say?"

"No."

"It doesn't look good for you, frankly," he continues, still looking at Roxie. "What I saw was you kneeling on a girl who has a broken arm and just had surgery last month. She's got four scratches, you've got one, and yours is not that bad." He fishes around in his drawer and, after a minute, pulls out a rectangular glass mirror, handing it to Roxie. "I don't think we want to take this to the principal, do we?"

"God, no. Please," I say.

Roxie looks at her scratch. I agree, it's not that bad. Mr. Polselli digs around a bit more in another drawer and hands her a small square packet containing an antiseptic wipe. He gives me one too.

Roxie sets the mirror on his desk out of my reach and glances at me. I avert my eyes and fold my arms as best I can with the cast. "Fine," she says. "Sorry."

Mr. Polselli looks at me, then picks up the mirror and hands it to me. "You don't want to go any further with this either?"

I train the mirror at my neck and study the scratches, four neat lines, the first three pretty heavy and the fourth just a light scratch like the one I gave Roxie. Thankfully, there's no dripping blood. It's going to be interesting explaining this one at home. "No, it's fine," I say. "Just a misunderstanding."

Mr. Polselli nods. "Okay, then." He scribbles a note on

a small pad of paper and hands it to Roxie.

She takes it. "Thanks," she says. And without another glance, she weaves through the aisle of students and goes out the door, eyes still shiny, biting her lip.

Mr. Polselli scribbles a note to get me back into class, and then he says, "She was on your stomach. Any need to get you checked out? You had some internal injuries from your crash, right?"

I smile, and now my eyes fill with tears because he's being nice, and because the danger and fear of the moment just caught up with me. "I'm okay. She wasn't pressing too hard or anything."

He looks down at his desk as a tear spills over the edge of my lower lid and I swipe it away. "Did you get your letter back?" he asks.

I freeze. "Yes."

He smiles. "Good." He hands me the excused note as the second bell rings and the students in his classroom start to sit down. "Take a few minutes to clean up. I added ten minutes to the excused time on your pass."

I take the pass and the antiseptic pad. "Thank you," I say. "A lot." And before another tear can leak out, I turn and barrel down the aisle, hoping nobody's looking at me and my big ol' neckful of scratches.

Seventeen

"Jeez," Trey says when he sees me at lunch. "What happened to you? Looks like Sawyer's got either a well-oiled hinge on that jaw or some retractable incisors."

I sit down next to Trey as Sawyer finds us and sits across from us.

"Random feline incident," I say, waving him off. "One of my fans got a little too close."

Sawyer examines my neck, then glances at Trey. "For the record, I did not do that." He looks at me. "Does it hurt? Any repercussions?"

"Yes, and no, thankfully. Polselli's cool. He kept it small. Good thing nobody threw a punch." I pull the crumpled note out of my pocket and hand it to Sawyer.

Trey swipes it.

"Seriously?" both Sawyer and I exclaim.

Trey stares at us like we're insane. "Calm down," he says. "Take a moment." He slowly hands the paper to Sawyer. "It's just a lingering adolescent attention-grabbing behavior. We all do it. It's human nature."

I start laughing softly, insanely, at the plate of lard-filled fats on the table in front of me.

"Trey," Sawyer says, and then he grabs my hand and squeezes it so I stop acting crazy.

I look up.

Trey's eyes narrow slightly. "Yes?"

"We—*I*—need your help."

Trey bats his eyelashes. "Oh?"

Sawyer flashes a grin despite the intensity of his thoughts. "No, not like that. It's, uh . . . God, this is going to sound insane, but—"

Trey grows serious again. "Oh, no." He leans forward. "Did you just say the magic word?"

"He did," I say.

Sawyer looks over his shoulder, making sure nobody's paying attention to us, and then he leans in. "Trey, ever since the crash, I—"

"No," Trey says. "Shit."

"Ever since the crash, I've been having this—"

"No." Trey sits back. "No, you haven't. No."

Sawyer sits back. "Yes."

Trey shakes his head. "Not funny. It's not quite April Fools' Day. Good practice joke, though." His mouth is strained. I know this look. It's the *I'm pretending I'm not freaked out right now* look. A classic Demarco face.

Sawyer digs the heels of his hands into his eyes and then rests his arms on the table and looks back at Trey. "I wish it was a joke."

Trey throws a nervous glance my way. I don't smile. He looks back at Sawyer. "No. You are mistaken. You are not having a vision. It's just PTSD or something. You've been through a lot."

Sawyer sighs. "Okay. Well. You would know." He stares at his lunch and shoves a forkful of by-product into his mouth. His eyes get glassy and he won't look at either of us. He chews a few times and then just stands up and takes his tray to the guys in dishwashing.

"He's serious?" Trey says.

"Yeah. Thanks for making him feel like crap."

"Fuck. What did you do to him?"

The guilt pang strikes again. I get up as Sawyer comes back this way. "Yeah, I don't know," I say. "Come on. We need to talk to him."

Trey sighs and gets up. "Okay." He grabs my tray and his and takes them away while I meet up with Sawyer.

"He knows you're serious now," I say.

Sawyer just shakes his head. "Maybe this was a bad idea."

"I don't think we have a choice. Let's just get it out there to him, see what he says. Please—I think he'll help us."

He presses his lips together. "Fine."

I beckon to Trey.

Trey catches up to us and we leave the cafeteria together. The clock says we've got about twelve minutes before the bell rings. We walk down to the trophy hallway, where only the memories of students linger—almost nobody hangs out here; they just pass through.

When we reach a quiet corner, Trey stops and faces us. "Okay, explain. How the hell did you start seeing a vision? What is this, some sort of contagion? A virus? What? It's like a bad B movie."

"We don't know. All I know is that I don't have my vision anymore, but Sawyer has one now."

"So what is it—a snowplow hitting *our* restaurant this time?"

I look at Sawyer. "You should explain everything. Including what you said in your note."

Sawyer begins. And I watch the two guys I love most in the world talk to each other. They are almost exactly the same height, a few inches taller than me. Trey's eyes are black and his hair is darker than Sawyer's, almost black, but they both have natural waves. Sawyer tries to fight his hair by keeping it short, while Trey coaxes his longer locks to curl every morning. I almost smile as I watch them. They are both so beautiful.

But the story Sawyer tells is not beautiful. I tune in, watching Trey's face go from shock to disbelief. "A school shooting," Trey says. "God, that's my worst nightmare." He shivers.

I didn't know that. "Mine's a toss-up between burning and being crushed," I murmur.

"Drowning," Sawyer adds. "Stampede. Or . . . being shot in the face by a fucking maniac or two."

That brings us back. "So we have two shooters now," I say, opening up the note Sawyer gave me this morning. Trey shushes me as a group of freshmen walk by. One of them eyes us in fear.

Sawyer waits until they're gone. "Yeah."

"And you don't know what school," Trey says. "That's . . . impossible."

"We need help, man. You're the only one who will believe us."

I watch conflict wash across Trey's face.

"Guys," he says, "look. I'm not trying to be all superior or grown up or whatever, but this is insane. *Insane.* How bad . . . I mean, the visions—I guess they're pretty bad."

"They let up a little when I manage to figure something out. But yeah. It's about fifty million times worse than having the theme song from 'Elmo's World' stuck in your head for a month straight."

Trey glances at the clock. "I think . . ." He gives me a guilty look, and then his gaze drops to the floor. "Look. I think it's too big for two teenagers. Or three. And, Sawyer, you should try and just get through it until it happens, and then hopefully it'll go away."

The bell rings.

"But, Trey," I say, "it's a lot of people. It's their families. Their lives."

"You don't know them."

"We don't know that for sure," I say, my voice pitching higher. "Besides, I feel like it's my fault. I mean, Sawyer didn't do anything to deserve this stupid vision, except somehow he caught it from me. I have to do something—" I grab his shirtsleeve as he turns to go to class. "Trey, come on."

"Come on, what? It's too dangerous. You're being irrational. I'm sorry about the noise in your head, Sawyer, and I hope it goes away soon, but, well, we almost died once already. If we manage to survive this, it won't be for long, because our parents will murder us." He starts walking quickly. "Get to class," he says over his shoulder to me.

Sawyer and I look at each other. "I'll work on him," I say.

"No. It's cool. I'll . . . I'll see you."

"I'm planning on the library if you can make it."

Sawyer's face sags. "I—I don't think so. Not today." He turns and goes toward his next class, and I go to sculpting. With Trey.

Eighteen

"Let's just talk about it a little more before you decide," I whisper once the teacher lets us loose to work on our own. Trey and I share a table, which is, according to our stunned classmates, something no brother and sister have ever before done willingly in the history of education. I don't get why not, but whatever.

Trey pretends I'm not there.

I don't know how to handle him when he does the silent treatment—it may be a stereotype, but we Italians aren't exactly known for our ability to keep our opinions quiet. All I know is that if I poke him a little, he'll start in on me, and that's when we can actually accomplish something.

"What if we *do* know one of the victims?" I whisper. "Does that change anything?"

He frowns at his misshapen bowl, then scrunches up his nose and smashes the clay into a ball and starts over.

I try again. "What if you save someone and he turns out to be the guy of your dreams?"

He turns toward me. "For shit's sake, Jules," he hisses. "This is not a romantic situation in any possible way. Grow up."

Yow. I stand abruptly and walk over to the paint shelf, pretending to pick out colors for the fake fruits I've been making to go in Trey's dumb lopsided bowl that he keeps destroying, all of which will one day be buried under a sea of bullshit crud collected by my father. I think about painting my fruit Day-Glo colors so they'll be easier to find when my mother's looking for something to put on top of my casket after I get shot to death. And then I start thinking about actually getting shot if things don't go well, and I really start creeping myself out.

I'm pulled back to reality when I realize somebody's calling my name. I whirl around, and it's the art teacher telling me and Trey to go to Dr. Grimm's office—the principal. Yeah, that's his real name. Thank dog he's not an oncologist.

Trey's puzzled glance meets mine, and then in an instant my heart clutches, because I realize if they want both of us it's not just because of my stupid scratchfest with Roxie. It's got to be something serious with Rowan or Mom or—or Dad. Fuck.

I stumble out of the room after Trey, and I feel like the world is coming up around my head like water. When we're alone in the hallway, both of us walking faster than normal, I say it. "Do you think Dad . . . did it?"

Trey's teeth are clenched and he replies in monotone. "I don't know."

How awesome is it being a kid who's always wondering if one day she's going to come home from school to find out her dad offed himself?

We round the corner near the office, and inside, through the glass wall, I see a cop. "Oh, Christ," I say, and I feel all the blood flooding out of my head. "Do you see Mom anywhere?"

"No."

We reach the door and Trey pushes it open and I stare at the cop and then at the secretary and I can't help it. "What's wrong?" I say, breathless. "Is Rowan here?"

The secretary, Miss Branderhorst, frowns at me like I did something wrong.

Trey whips his head around as somebody enters the office behind us.

It's Sawyer.

He looks as puzzled as we are.

The cop asks us our names, and then the principal comes

out, and they make us go back into his office, and the only thing I can think of is that my dad went postal and took out Sawyer's parents and *then* killed himself. *Mom,* I think, and now I'm freaking myself out and telling myself to calm down.

We sit in chairs, and none of our parents are there, most likely because they're dead, and then the cop says, "Where were you at lunch today?" And this is weird, but right then I realize he's the guy who fills in once a week for our regular beat cop, Al, by the restaurant, and somehow knowing that makes me feel better.

"Wait." Sawyer holds his hand out. "Um, did somebody die? Why are we here?"

Principal Grimm interjects. "Mr. Angotti, kindly answer the question."

Trey sits up, his eyes sparking. "You're not going to tell us if somebody died?"

"Nobody died," the cop says.

"Jeeezabel," I say, slumping back in relief. "You gave us a heart attack."

The cop and Principal Grimm exchange a look. And then the cop repeats the question. "Where were you at lunch today?"

"We ate lunch in the cafeteria. Together," Trey says. "And then we wandered the halls until the next period started like everybody always does. Are we in trouble or something?"

The cop looks at me. "What did you talk about?"

"What?" I ask, confused as hell, and then my blood runs cold. Somebody overheard something. I sense Trey stiffening in the chair next to me.

"We received a 911 call from a student who says he overheard you three talking about something suspicious. Do you want to tell me what you were talking about?"

I keep the puzzled look on my face. "Let's see, we talked about the weather warming up, we talked about our work schedules—me and Trey at Demarco's Pizzeria, and Sawyer at Angotti's Trattoria—" I add, in case it helps. "And, gosh, I don't know," I say, looking at the boys on either side of me. "My psych project, maybe? TV shows, video games?" I start throwing out random things, hoping one of them will save me.

"Call of Duty," Sawyer says. "You ever play?" He looks at the cop. "It's kind of violent, but . . ."

The cop doesn't answer. He looks at me and my cast, and then at the scratches I almost forgot I have on my neck. "You're the Demarco kids who saved this guy's parents' restaurant," he says, flicking a thumb at Sawyer.

"Yes," Trey says. "Well, it was mostly Jules."

I blush appropriately, for once. "You're our beat cop when Al has his days off, aren't you?" I ask.

"Police officer," Principal Grimm corrects.

The cop grins for the first time, rolls his eyes without

the principal seeing. He pockets his little notebook and adjusts the gun on his belt. "Yeah, I'm your fill-in beat cop," he says to me, and then he turns to the principal. "I think we're done here."

The principal's eyes flicker, but he nods. "Thank you, Officer Bentley."

The cop leaves, and then the principal looks at us. He clasps his hands together. "Well. You may go."

We all stand up and file out to the reception area. Principal Grimm flags down Miss Branderhorst to write us excuses to get back into class.

Once we're in the hallway and my heart starts beating again, I let out a staggered breath. I don't dare say anything or even look at Trey and Sawyer. When we turn the corner, Sawyer puts his arm over my shoulders, and then Trey puts his arm over my shoulders and Sawyer's arm, and I reach around both of their waists, and we don't talk. Not a word.

Except for when Trey says, "All right. I'm in. But only to keep you bozos from getting killed."

Nineteen

After school Trey and Sawyer head to the library while I drive Rowan home.

She observes me loftily. "Are you going to tell me what happened to your neck?"

My fingers automatically reach up to touch the scratches. "Oh. Stupid Roxie took something and I accidentally scratched her trying to get it back, so she lunged at me and scratched the hell out of my neck."

"Wow. Well, I guess she's probably jealous."

I raise an eyebrow, check my speedometer, touch the brakes just slightly. "Of what?"

"Come on," Rowan says. "Pay attention for once. She's been in love with Sawyer for years."

"Years? How would you know?"

"The same way you sophomores know more about the junior class than you know about the freshman class. Everybody watches up."

I'm a little surprised at how delicious this news feels. "I thought they were just friends."

"Please. Is *anyone* just friends? There are always other motivating factors in relationships. Maybe not constant, but consistent."

I look at her.

She looks back at me, her face certain.

I shrug, wondering how she became such a philosopher all of a sudden.

"So now what?" Rowan says.

"Now what what?"

"Now what are you guys doing? You, Trey. Sawyer. Something's up."

"Nothing. Don't worry about it."

She flips the visor down and examines her face. "My flight is Sunday morning," she says. She rummages through her backpack and pulls out a pair of tweezers, then starts plucking invisible hairs from her perfect eyebrows.

I haven't thought about her flight. Or about her secret visit to see Charlie. I haven't thought about her at all lately.

She continues. "So I'll need a ride to O'Hare Airport while Mom and Dad are at mass." She's never flown before, and she says it like she's bored.

"Impeccable timing. When do you come back?"

"I'll be back Friday before dinner service. You're welcome."

I laugh. Sometimes Rowan just leaves me speechless. "Okay," I say. "What do you want me to, like, *say* to Mom and Dad when they get home from mass to find their youngest child missing? I mean, can I tell them the truth? Are you going to give me all the information about where you'll be and stuff?"

"I'll have my cell phone with me. That's all they need to know. But yeah, I'll give you the address and stuff too in case Charlie is secretly an ax murderer. But don't give it to them. Please." She licks her pinkie and smooths her eyebrows, then deposits the tweezers back into her bag as I turn down the alley behind our home and park a few buildings away so nobody sees me—I don't want my dad to force me to come inside. "Maybe we can talk tonight." She gets out and waves, then saunters down the alley toward the restaurant like she owns the world.

And I totally want to be her.

I meet Trey and Sawyer at the library. They're up in the loft on the corner couches where you can see everyone approaching but still have a private conversation. I plop down next to Sawyer, kick off my shoes, and curl up into him, and he slips an arm around my shoulders and kisses the top of my head. And I feel like this exact moment right here, this feeling of warmth and love, is what I have been waiting for my entire life.

Trey watches us. He smiles a small smile and doesn't look away. And then he sighs and leans forward, elbows on his knees, and says, "All right. Number one: Nobody here gets hurt." At first I think he must have new information from Sawyer that I haven't heard yet, but then I realize it's a command.

Sawyer nods. "I hear you, bro. We hear you. No crazy stunts. No matter what."

"Of course," I agree.

While I was gone, Sawyer filled Trey in on a few of the minor but important details—the tree, the grass, the tiny stop sign, the old building with ivy on it.

I pull the note Sawyer gave me this morning out of my pocket and hold it out. "We need to destroy this or something," I say. "Yours, too."

Sawyer pulls his note out and takes mine. "We have a shredder in the office. I'll take care of it. From now on, only verbal communication, and we don't talk about g-u-n-s in school. Does Trey know about your secret phone?"

Trey raises an eyebrow.

"It's just a temporary throwaway," Sawyer says. "Don't bother trying to text her."

I give Trey my new cell number and watch him enter it

into his phone. "Sawyer, can you get away from the proprietors long enough to drive by some schools? The list is in your hand—can you memorize them before you shred that?"

"Yeah," Sawyer says. "I'll drive around tonight and tomorrow morning before school." He looks at the addresses. "Some of these are way out there."

"Are you safe to drive?"

"So far." Sawyer squinches his eyelids shut and rubs them. "The vision keeps playing in the windows down there, though, and it's giving me a headache." He points to the wall of glass on the main floor below us. "And in the face of that clock." There's an old school clock on the wall opposite our couch.

"What about your windshield and mirrors?" I ask, worried, knowing how distracting that is, and how much worse it could be for Sawyer going out into city traffic.

"Not bad," he says lightly. "But . . . things are getting worse. The noise is driving me insane. I think—I feel like it's happening very soon."

Trey lifts his head. "I'll go with you to look at schools," he says. "I'll drive."

I bite my lip. I want to go, but I haven't been pulling my weight at the restaurant. "That's a great idea," I say. I glance outside and then at the clock. "Maybe you guys should go now before it gets dark. Do the close ones. It's rush hour."

Trey gets up and blows out a sigh. "If we're going to do this, let's do it hard, fast, and often."

"Dot-com," I mutter, getting up. "Okay, be safe." I give them each a hug. "Talk it through from the beginning, maybe. Trey might have some good questions that will trigger something—anything—about day, time, place. Maybe identifying features of the . . ." I almost say "shooters," but now I'm scared to use the word. "Bad guys," I say. And that triggers my memory. "Oh," I say, turning to Sawyer. "Can you zoom in on a close-up of the, ah, weapon *and* the whiteboard? I'm not sure if the weapon's information will help anything, but I thought of it earlier when Officer Bentley was at school. I could see a logo on his. Is there a way to trace something like that? Or, like, figure out how many bullets a . . . thing . . . can shoot just by looking at it?"

Sawyer looks at me with this face dotted with little hints of surprise—in his eyes, the corners of his lips. "Good one, gorgeous," he says. "I'll check them both out in slo-mo tonight when I get home and I'll call you."

Big sigh.

And a question. Why does danger make love so much more intense?

Twenty

I hit the computers after Trey and Sawyer are gone so I can do my tree research, and my best guess is that the bush-tree in Sawyer's vision is a redbud. I pay to print a few pages of examples and take off. I make it home before five and get to the restaurant early to help set up for dinner.

"How was your tree research?" Dad booms when I glide through the kitchen. He looks good today. Clean shaven, a smile on his face. At school a few hours ago I thought he might have killed himself, but staring at him now, it's hard to imagine he's ever depressed.

"Good. Successfully identified a redbud tree. But teachers are hitting hard with assignments. I'm going to have to spend more time at school and at the library, where I can use decent computers." I cringe, hoping he doesn't see that as a slam, because it's just a fact. Our computer sucks. And I need to establish that I'm going to be gone more. But bringing up chess club again is a bad idea.

He lets it go. Even makes a joke about typewriters. Today he is my favorite kind of dad. I realize just how seldom this dad comes out these days, and I wonder what triggers it. When I catch a glimpse of Rowan, I know my dad's up days are numbered. As soon as he realizes what she's doing, it's going to be shitty again.

Part of me wants to tell them what she's up to. But I can't. I owe her. I owe her big, and she is well aware of that. In fact, she probably planned it that way. I shake my head and watch Rowan with new respect. She arrives on time every day. She kisses Mom and Dad on the cheek when she sees them, and greets Tony the cook like he's family. She tells them just enough about her day that they never say "You never tell us anything" to her. She treats everyone with respect and she's the one who gets the most customer love on the restaurant comment cards.

And it's all a big screen. A ruse. Well, that's not really fair to say, because she truly is a thoughtful, respectful, punctual person. But she also knows how to use her strengths to her advantage, and when she goes to New York, Mom and Dad are going to be absolutely gobsmacked—they'll never see it coming. Because if anything, Mom and Dad are looking at me to be the one to disappoint them again.

She's a freaking genius.

With Dad working at 100 percent tonight, Mom sends all three of us upstairs early. I grab Trey and drag him into his room, which is mildly messy. He has posters of famous people on his walls and weird gadget-like stuff between the books on his bookshelves.

I close the door. "Well?"

"Nothing. We got to three of the schools on your list before dark, and I thought of another one on the way home, but none of them looked right."

I flop down on his unmade bed. "Crap."

"He's picking me up at dark thirty and we're going to try to get out to Lake View and Lincoln Park and back before school starts."

"Ugh, that's going to be horrible at that hour."

He shrugs and sits next to me. "We don't have a choice. He thinks we're running out of time."

We both lie back on the bed and stare at his ceiling. "Anything new?"

"Still no. I asked him some questions that he thought he could find answers to in the vision." He sighs.

"Thanks for doing that."

"No, it's cool. He's a great guy."

I smile and look over at his face. "You sure you're not in love with him?"

That gets a laugh. "I'm in love with something, I guess, but not Sawyer, though I still think he's a total hottie. I guess I'm in love with this cute little relationship thing you guys have." His lingering smile is wistful. "And, like, you know, Rowan and . . . what's his name?"

"Charlie."

"Yeah, Charlie. I heard more about him the other day when I drove Rowan home. Seems like they've got something good too."

My throat catches a little. "You'll have it too. You will. I mean, maybe just not in high school. Maybe college. For sure college—things will be better."

He folds his hands behind his head. "I hope so, Jules. I really do."

There's a soft knock at his door.

"Come in," he hollers.

Rowan peeks her head in. "Hi. I heard my name and came running." She comes in and closes the door. She wrinkles up her nose and sniffs tentatively as she surveys Trey's mild clutter, and then she approaches the bed.

I sit up and shove Trey over so Rowan can sit too. "The only way you could have heard your name is if you were standing with your ear pressed against the door."

"It was a short run," she says agreeably.

My eyes grow wide and meet Trey's alarmed look. What else did she hear?

She sits down and lies back on the bed next to me. "So, guys," she says. "Isn't it about time you fill me in on this whole vision thing?"

Twenty-One

"Um," Trey says.

"Um," I say, and then add in a weak voice, "What?" I lie back down again.

She sighs. "Oh, please. Just come out with it already." She looks at her cell phone clock. "I'm leaving in a few days."

"Maybe we should talk about *that*," Trey says.

"Nice try." She sits up and scoots back so that she can lean against the wall between Trey's posters of Johnny Depp and Adele.

I tilt my head back so I'm looking at Rowan upside down. "What exactly do you think you know?"

"Well, I know you have a phone, I know you talk to Sawyer at night when you think I'm sleeping, I know somebody's having a vision of some kind of . . . shooting, and you all seem to think you have to do something about it."

Trey snorts and sits up. "Well, that about sums it up, Ro." He shakes his head, laughing. "Thank you and good night, everyone—I've got an early morning, so, uh, Jules? You wanna take this one in your office?"

I just stare dumbfounded at Rowan.

"Oh!" Trey adds, standing and fishing inside the pocket of his jeans. He pulls out a familiar key chain. "Just remembered. Great news. Dad says it's time to start advertising at school again." He gives me a patronizing smile and hands the keys to the new meatball truck to me. "Don't crash it. Have a ball."

"Har har. Don't forget my ten bucks," I mutter, taking the keys, and then I get up and shuffle toward the door, dragging Rowan by her pajama collar. "Come on, you little weasel," I say. "Girls' quarters. Immediately."

Mom and Dad are still in the restaurant. Ro and I go into our room and close the door. Rowan pulls her terry cloth robe from the closet, rolls it up, and presses it against the crack under the door as a sound barrier. I stand at the closet, take off my clothes, and put on some booty shorts and my "Peace, Love, Books" shirt, which I got from this dope bookshop called Anderson's. Ever since the visions, I started wearing it to bed because it made me feel calm, and bed plus calm equals sleep. Which I can always use more of.

Rowan turns out the light so when our parents come upstairs there's no chance of them seeing any light through the door cracks and barging in, and we climb into her bed. I lie on my side and sling my arm over her waist like I used to do when we were younger, and we talk about what the hell she's about to do.

"I guess I want to meet him," I say. I feel like the mom.

She's quiet for a moment. "Well, come to the library during second hour, then. Tomorrow. I'm always in that little study room with the door shut."

"I have class."

Rowan sighs. "Honestly, Jules. You're supposed to be the bad child."

"What, you want me to skip class? They'll call home."

"Not if you have a note from Mom."

"Right, and that'll be easy."

"Oh, Jules. Tsk."

"What, you forge her signature too? Do you even go to class at all?"

"I'm pretty good at it, actually."

I shake my head in Rowan's pillow and almost laugh. "One day you are going to get so busted."

"Nope," she says. "Because I have you taking the focus away."

"At least you admit it."

"Why wouldn't I? I'm nothing if not grateful."

I pinch her upper inner arm in the soft spot that hurts about fifty times more than it should, and she stifles a yelp and jabs her elbow into my boob.

"Ow, loser," I mutter.

We nurse our injuries. "Okay, fine," I say. "Write me a note and I'll find you."

"In my mind it's already written," she says.

"Okay, Gandhi."

"That was Yoda."

"Not even close."

"Yeah, well, I'm a little young for *Star Wars*."

"You're a little young for having a long-distance boyfriend."

"*You're* a little young for stalking a serial killer."

"It—he—they're not serial killers," I say. "It's a school shooting." I spend the next ten minutes giving her the whole explanation of the past months, including my crash vision and how everything happened with that, and everything that's now happening with Sawyer.

And she just listens and doesn't seem surprised or incredulous or anything. All she says is "I wonder what the shooters' motivation is?"

"So you believe it?" I ask.

"Why wouldn't I? You, Trey, and Sawyer can't all be nuts."

What a relief.

Later, when I'm in my own bed, falling asleep while waiting for Sawyer to call me, Rowan whispers, "Jules?"

I open my eyes and stare at the blinking neon light on the wall. "Yeah?"

"You said Sawyer thinks it's happening soon, right? And the weather forecast has the snow gone by early next week?"

"Yeah."

"Next week is spring break for *all* public schools around here. Nobody's in school. Every classroom in Chicago will be empty."

My heart clutches and I suck in a breath. And then my pillow starts vibrating.

Twenty-Two

"Hey," Sawyer says, his voice a husky whisper that slides down my spine. "Sorry it's so late. Did I wake you?"

"No, Rowan and I were just talking."

"Hi from me."

I look up and see Rowan propped up on one elbow in the dim light. "He says hi."

She grins, and then falls back on her bed and puts her pillow over her face and says, muffled, "Go ahead and do your oogy talk, I can't hear you."

I breathe out a laugh and put my mouth against the phone again. "Rowan knows," I say.

He hesitates. "Um, okay . . . ?"

"She was onto us for a while. Don't worry, she's good

with it. And she just discovered something big for us."

"Oh. Well, in that case, cool. What?"

"If this thing happens early next week, or anytime next week, it won't happen at a public school because we're all on spring break at the same time."

He's silent, and for a minute I think I lost the connection. And then, "Well. Damn. How did we not think of that?"

"Fresh ears and eyes are good," I say, remembering. "And don't worry about her. She keeps more secrets than a tomb."

"I'm not worried," he says, and his voice totally has me convinced that he's got this whole thing under control. But I know better.

"So that leaves private schools?" he asks.

"That seems to be the logical conclusion, though I imagine some of them have the same spring break as us."

"How many private schools are there?"

"I'm not sure. But instead of wasting time in the morning going to check out the two public schools you were planning to look at, maybe we three can meet somewhere to do research?"

"Four," Rowan says, still muffled.

"I thought you couldn't hear me," I whisper.

"What?" Sawyer says.

"Nothing. I mean, Rowan wants to help, if it's cool with you."

"Hell yes. I'll take all the help I can get. Meet me at the coffee shop, North and Twenty-Fifth. Five thirty?"

"Sure." I turn to Rowan. "You're in. We're leaving here at five fifteen in the morning. Don't be late."

She lifts her arm from the blankets and gives a thumbs-up.

I turn away from her and face my wall. "We're going to figure this out," I say, softer.

He's quiet. I picture him in his bed, nodding.

"Jules," he whispers.

"Yeah?"

"Thank you."

I smile. "Sure."

"Jules?"

"Yeah?"

"I wish you were here with me so I could hold you."

My eyes close and a wave of longing rises through me. I remember middle school and my Sawyer pillow. "Hold your pillow. Pretend it's me. I'm here. Right here with you."

I hear a muffled sound like he's actually doing what I suggested, which almost brings tears to my eyes, because what guy does that?

"Jules," he says once more.

"Yeah?" I say again.

He's quiet for a long time. And then he says, "I'm really very insanely much in love with you."

And I can't speak, because this big ball of tears and air is blocking my words, and finally I sniffle and I manage to squeak out, "That is the best thing anybody has ever said to me, ever. And I am insanely really very much in love with you, too."

We sit on the phone all quiet for a minute.

And then, from below Rowan's pillow, a snicker.

I freeze. And she snorts.

I twist around. "Oh my God, Rowan, shut *up*, I hate you!" I grab my pillow and chuck it at her head, but her bed doesn't stop shaking until after Sawyer and I hang up.

In the morning I stumble out of bed at four thirty and kick Rowan in the butt to wake her up. Trey is just emerging from the steamy bathroom when I get there, and he looks at me with surprise.

"What's up?" he whispers. "You going with us?"

I tell him Rowan's discovery and our latest plan. He gets out of my way so I can take a quick shower. Forty-eight minutes later we three are headed out into the darkness.

When we get to the coffee shop, Sawyer's got a table staked out and is leaning over his laptop. We join him.

I look at Rowan. "Spinach-and-feta wrap and a tall coffee, blacker than black," I say.

Rowan nods primly and turns to Sawyer. "May I take your order?"

He gets a cute puzzled grin on his face. "Iced coffee and a sausage-and-egg sandwich." He reaches for his wallet.

Rowan puts her hand out to stop him. "That won't be necessary," she says. She looks at Trey. "Well? What would you like?" Her tone is annoyed.

"What's going on?" Trey asks.

Rowan looks at me.

I shrug. "Tell him."

She clears her throat, clearly not wanting to tell. "I'm buying everyone breakfast today on account of how I disrespected Jules's love."

Sawyer chokes and Trey laughs out loud. "I see. Well, in that case, I'll have a hot vanilla chai tea, yogurt, and granola. With whipped cream. On everything. And a brownie. And—okay, I guess that's enough."

Rowan gives me a condescending sneer and I respond with my superior smile. She goes up to the counter.

Sawyer recovers and starts typing again. I pull my chair closer so I can see, and Trey looks around the other side of him. "There's a ton of private schools," he says under his breath.

"The oldest schools might be mostly Catholic around old Chicago," I say.

"Here's one, Saint Patrick. Over a hundred and fifty years old," Trey says.

Sawyer pulls up the map and zooms in until he has

a street view. "Nope. The building is wrong." He looks up at me. "You know, you might be onto something. The scene of the building in the vision has a tall section. Reminded me of a church." He digs further, and Trey and I keep track of the schools he rules out. Then he finds a list of private schools by neighborhood all within the city limits. There are dozens of them.

It's frustrating. "We need a better computer at home," I say. "This is crazy. I think we're the only kids in the entire city who don't have laptops." I drum my fingers on the table.

Sawyer gently places his hand over mine, stilling my fingers, but his eyes never leave the screen and his other hand moves swiftly around the keyboard. "We can go to school at seven when the doors open and try—" He shakes his head. "Oh, that's right. We're not breathing, typing, or speaking a word of this there."

Rowan finally comes back with a tray of food, then retraces her steps and returns with the coffees.

She joins us as we work and eat, and sits quietly, respecting our love, listening as we talk through the various options and why they don't fit the puzzle in front of us. When seven o'clock rolls around and it's time to head over to school, we have nothing.

Nobody talks as the four of us walk into school, dejected shoulder to dejected shoulder: Trey, Rowan, me,

Sawyer. As we reach the freshman hallway, Rowan peels away from our sad little group, but not before shoving a folded note into my hand.

"Second hour," she says. And then she frowns. "Put some makeup on or something, sheesh."

Twenty-Three

Five things Rowan rocks at:
1. Writing fake notes from our mother
2. Disrespecting my love
3. Being on time
4. Flying under the radar
5. Picking gorgeous boyfriends

There are many things Charles Broderick Banks is not. He is not Italian. He's not grumpy. He's not hard on the eyes. He's also not American born. He's South African–Irish-English, he says. The lilt in his voice is swoony. No wonder Rowan is in love.

Rowan and I huddle at a cubicle computer desk, and I take him in: his deep umber eyes, his sun-bleached blond hair, and his tanned, lightly freckled skin that makes him look as if he just came home from a trip to the tropics. He has an adorable little scar on his head that looks like an inch-long part in his hair. His smile is warm and sweet, and I watch my little sister's face come to life when she talks to him. He and Rowan chitchat awkwardly at first with me there, but soon they are bantering back and forth.

He seems to know only the nice things about me, and he asks me pointed questions. "How's your arm? Do you get your cast off soon?"

"Soon," I say. "Next week. It doesn't hurt at all anymore. I practically forget it's here except when I need to, you know, bend that wrist or something."

He grins. "Rowan says you're very brave."

I blush. "Oh, really?" I glance at her and she smirks.

"She's also very mean," Rowan offers. "She made me buy everyone breakfast this morning."

"I'm sure you deserved it," he says.

"Okay, I approve of this boy," I say.

"Approved!" he says, doing an English version of the Target Lady from *Saturday Night Live*. And then he turns his head away from the camera, distracted by a distant voice.

I look at Rowan. "Uh-oh? Or no?"

She shakes her head and listens. "No, it's his tutor.

Oops, my bad. It's his mom." She watches for a second until a tall blond woman appears. "Hi, Mom B!" She waves at the screen.

"Hey, Ro," the woman says. She's wearing designer workout clothes drenched in sweat but still somehow manages to look gorgeous and radiant. "Who's this?"

I wave weakly. "Hi, um, I'm Rowan's sister."

"Oh, Jules. Cool—heard a lot about you."

I nod and smile. *So it seems.*

"We're excited to see Rowan again. Thank your mom and dad for us—I left a message the other day but I know they're really busy."

I glance at Rowan as her face turns red. The little weasel erased it, I'll bet.

Mrs. Banks continues. "We'll be waiting at Baggage Claim, and it's a direct flight so there's no way she'll get stranded somewhere. Just follow the signs to Baggage Claim, hon."

"And I'll call you when I land," Rowan says, like they've rehearsed this.

"And me," I say.

"Yes, I'll call you, too."

Charlie gives his mom a look, and she waves. "Okay, gotta go. See you Sunday."

Rowan calls out her good-bye, and she and Charlie share a private joke I don't get, and they're all just . . .

carefree and having fun, and the biggest stress weighing on them is wondering if rain will delay the flight.

I sit back in my chair, working my fingers through a tangle in my hair, and just watch them. And I can't wait to have so few worries. I can't wait to have fun again. I can't wait to have that kind of light, easy banter with the guy I love.

After a while I excuse myself to let them do their mushy talk in private, ahem. On the walk back to class, I find myself wondering if something horrible will happen while Rowan is gone. Worrying that my parents won't know where to find her or how to contact her. I clench my jaw and force the thought away. Because that can't happen. It can't and it won't.

My stomach hurts.

Twenty-Four

At lunch we don't talk about anything much. We all just sort of sit there feeling glum. Sawyer holds his spoon in front of him, staring at it.

"It's in your spoon?" I ask.

He nods. "It's upside down, though, because of the scientific nature of spoon reflections or whatever."

Trey grunts like he knows what that's called, but he doesn't offer up a term, and I don't care enough at this moment to put forth the effort to ask. Instead, I ask the broken-record question, "Do you see anything new?"

"Actually . . ." Sawyer trails off and keeps looking at the spoon. "Hm."

I sit up, watching him, and Trey raises an eyebrow.

"It's weird," Sawyer says. "My eyes focus on different parts of it than they did before. I think . . . I think . . ."

Roxie and BFF Sarah come up to the table. "Admiring your reflection?" Roxie asks. Her neck scratch is practically gone. Mine are still ugly. They stay hidden under my collar.

Sawyer doesn't look up, so Roxie sticks her boobs out, being way obvious, and I almost laugh at how stupid it is to do that, like a peacock making sure everybody sees his feathers. Only they're not beautiful, colorful feathers, they're just boobs. Trey actually does laugh, in a snorty fashion, and he rolls his eyes. But he can get away with that. He's a senior. He has nothing to fear from her.

Sawyer turns his head and looks at Roxie's boobs, seeing as how they're practically in his face, and, well, because he's a guy. He wears a slightly bewildered look and then raises his eyes to meet Roxie's. "Oh, hey," he mumbles. "What's up?" He scoots his chair over so he doesn't actually get an eye poked out, and he glances at me with a worried expression like he thinks I might punch him in the face.

Body language is so interesting, isn't it? We're learning about it in Mr. Polselli's class. I observe. Roxie takes the tiniest step back and her shoulders relax. "Not much. Just haven't seen you in a while." The boobs deflate slightly, which makes me stop worrying about one of them accidentally bursting. And neither Roxie nor BFF Sarah so much as glances at me, but they both look at Trey and Sawyer. I smile at Sawyer when he catches my eye, and he relaxes. And it's weird. I think I'm supposed to be jealous, but I'm not. I don't think I'm very good at being a stereotypical girl.

"I've been pretty busy," Sawyer says coolly. He shrugs and takes a small bite of his burger. "Attack anyone today?"

"Well, let me tell you," Roxie says, ignoring his disdain. She shoves her butt against Sawyer in an attempt to get him to slide over so she can share the edge of his chair. He stops chewing but doesn't move over, leaving Roxie and her butt hovering weirdly. I just keep watching, and it's like I'm invisible or something. Like I'm not even there. I glance at Trey, who is now finishing up his lunch and ignoring the girls.

"Can you see me?" I ask him.

He looks. Narrows his eyes. "Only if I squint really hard."

I nod. "That's what I thought."

"It's kind of a cool superpower, if you ask me. Invisibility."

"Yeah, you know? You're right. Right, Roxie?"

No response.

"I don't think she can hear invisible people," Trey says.

I shrug. "So that's two superpowers for me, if you really think about it."

Trey chugs down the rest of his iced tea and wipes his mouth with his napkin. "I'll give you that."

"Thanks."

"Who's the other one again?"

I glance up. "That's BFF Sarah."

"BFF is her first name?"

"Ah . . . yes. Yes, it is."

"Interesting."

"Not much different from a name like J.T. or R.J. or C.J."

"Except there's no J."

"True."

Sarah turns sharply and frowns at us. "You guys are beyond weird."

My eyes open wide. "You can see me?"

She shakes her head, disgusted, and tugs at Roxie, who, after being denied, is now leaning over the table, talking to Sawyer about Spring Fling, which is like prom but not really, because it's only for freshmen and sophomores and it's lame.

"So you want to go with me?" Roxie asks him. "I got my license. I'll pick you up."

"Um . . . Rox . . ."

"It'll be like old times, you know? We can make out behind the bleachers like when we were a couple." She's speaking really loudly. And finally the jealous factor kicks in. And it kicks in hard. Because I don't know what she's talking about.

"Roxie, what the heck—" Sawyer begins, and I hear anger in his voice.

I stand up and push my chair back, the heat rising to my face.

Trey touches my arm. "I think we need to just sit and watch this, don't you?"

BFF Sarah crosses her arms, bored.

Roxie smiles at Sawyer.

Sawyer looks at me, his lips parted, eyes apologetic. "Please don't go," he says.

I sit down again. "Yeah," I say to Trey, "you're right."

But I can't concentrate on what anybody else is saying right now, because all I see is Sawyer and Roxie making out behind the bleachers. And I feel like a stupid fool. Because I thought somehow Sawyer would have waited for me like I waited for him. I thought our first kiss was our first kiss. And it's not; it was just my first. And even though it's ridiculous for me to expect that he hasn't kissed anybody else, because we're sixteen, for crying out loud, it still makes my throat ache.

When I can focus, I watch BFF Sarah grow impatient and walk away.

And I see Sawyer's mouth moving, and Roxie scowling and getting angry. But I can't comprehend anything.

After a minute, I look at Trey. "I really need to go," I say in a low voice.

"If you leave now, she'll feel like she won something. Just stay here and talk to me. Ignore them. She's looking to get a rise out of you, so don't let her. You and Sawyer will work this out. He's a good guy, remember?"

"I know." But he made out with Roxie. He was a *couple* with her. How did I not know this? Maybe because I'm a freaking outcast, huh? Pretty stinking likely.

"So, about that other thing," Trey says, keeping my gaze locked on his. "Let's meet up after school and do the library again. I need to do some research for a term paper anyway. Sound good?"

"Sure," I say, my voice hollow. They're talking about me now. I stare at Trey, and he keeps talking. And then he laughs, and I think it's because Roxie just suggested Sawyer was gay and having a secret relationship with Trey, and I was acting as his beard. I can't help it—I have to tune in.

Sawyer looks hard at Roxie for a long moment. And then he says, "Yes, okay, I admit it. I'm gay, and I'm in love with Trey."

Roxie stares at him. "You are not."

"You just said I was. And, well, it's true."

"I made out with a *gay*?"

The immediate area goes silent. Heads turn, everybody looking to see who the newly outed gay guy is. I hate this. I glance at Trey, who seems to be enjoying this immensely.

"Well, I'm not just any old *gay*, I'm Sawyer the gay." His lip twitches. "That's what we call each other."

"True story," Trey adds. "But I rejected him."

"He did, yes. Multiple times, in fact."

"But he's still very much in love with me, and I like that, because it kind of feels like I have power over him. It's a form of torture, and it's fun."

Sawyer nods. Then he shakes his head. "Not fun for me, I mean. For him."

A few people around us start snickering.

Roxie's face turns red. I think she figured out they're teasing her and sort of throwing her own actions in her face, but she says through gritted teeth, "So are you gay or not?"

Sawyer drops the shtick. "Really? You're asking me this?"

"Obviously."

Sawyer gives her an incredulous look. "Okay, well, then I . . . I am."

Her eyes bulge. "Were you gay when we made out?"

Sawyer holds his straight face. "Not before, but after . . . well, then I was."

A few people laugh, and Roxie falters, and I feel sorry for her. Not because she's gullible. But because it means so damn much to her to know if she made out with *a gay*.

"Okay, that's enough, guys," I mutter.

The bell rings. People around us turn back to gather their stuff. Trey squeezes my shoulder and slips away. Roxie stomps off, and I stand there, looking across the table at Sawyer, who is searching my face with his eyes. And I don't know what to say, except "I guess I'll see you at the library after school."

He sighs and looks down at the table. "Yeah. Okay."

I stand there a second more, and then I take my tray away. I have to run to make it to class on time.

Twenty-Five

And here's the thing. I hate that junk. I hate that whole whatever you want to call it—the misunderstanding-slash-thing-between-us story line. It's on every TV show, in every book you read, every movie. Something always happens to put this stupid wedge in the budding relationship, and the people don't talk about it so they just keep being misunderstood, and by the end of the movie, maybe it all works out and maybe it doesn't, but I hate it and I wish this kind of crap didn't happen. Why can't the two lovers just be together? Why can't the fucking *plot* of the fucking *story* of everybody's *life* just be like, hey, you finally find the person you want to *be* with, and you just be with them, and that part is the good part? And the conflict is something else, like a crash and an explosion, or a school shooting, but you're just still together with that person as a team and you both fight *together* against some *other* enemy? Why does this have to happen? Because it's very clear to me that we just. Don't. Need this. Right now.

"So, uh, that got a little out of hand," Trey says when he gets to our table in sculpting class. "Sorry about that. It was all in fun."

"I know."

"Why are you being so quiet?"

"I'm not sure."

He nods, and we sit there in silence for once, working side by side making a bowl and painting fruit, both of us knowing that scary junk is coming, and the world is so much bigger than this place, and these people, and a stupid rivalry.

We meet up at the library after school and Trey wisely goes to look for books for his research project, leaving me and Sawyer alone on the couch in the library loft.

And the dude, to his credit, looks way more distraught about what happened at lunch than he is over the visions that are driving him crazy. "I'm sorry I never told you I made out with Roxie," he says. "We were never a couple, I don't care what she says. We made out twice at the beginning of ninth grade, more just to experience things and mess around."

I listen and say, "You didn't have to disclose any of that to me, you know. People have pasts. It's not a big deal. I mean, I guess my reaction was more because of the way she was approaching it, and approaching, um, you. And just pretending I wasn't there and throwing it in my face."

"Boobs first?" He laughs.

I smile. "Yeah, you noticed? It's kind of sad, actually."

He nods. "She has no self-confidence. And . . . I think I took the joke too far. I kept expecting her to get it, but she got so hung up on whether she'd—well, yeah. You were there."

"Yeah." I shrug. "Well, thanks for explaining, and, you know, I'm not mad or anything, I just don't like her. She used to be my friend and now she's just . . . sad. And mean."

"So . . . you still like me?" he asks with a grin. He slips his hand in mine.

"A little," I agree.

By the time Trey comes back, Sawyer and I are both on computers. I'm researching private schools; Sawyer's trying to get close-ups of every frame in his vision. "When I was watching it in my spoon and everything was upside down," he says, "I thought I saw something through the window."

Trey looks at Sawyer's screen automatically, even though he and I both know we can't see anything. He laughs. "You picked 'Surprised Kitty' as the video to channel it?"

Sawyer is concentrating too hard to laugh. "Yeah. I mean, why not entertain you guys?" He hits pause and stares, then takes a screen shot that only he can see and starts enlarging it.

I go back to looking up schools and start bookmarking them so I can show them all to Sawyer at once. And then he mutters, "Yesss," and starts scribbling things on a notepad. "There's the road in relationship to the building. Now I'm getting a bigger picture."

Trey and I look over and wait for him to finish. We haven't had a "Yesss" in forever. I squeeze my eyes shut and hope for a major breakthrough.

But when I open my eyes again, I see Trey looking at his phone and muttering, "Shit," and I see Sawyer looking at the stairway and getting to his feet.

Because guess who's here? Yay, it's my dad.

Dad reaches the top of the stairs and spies us. Trey types something quickly and stashes his phone, and he stands up, so I stand up too.

"Hey, Dad," Trey says. He puts his hands in his pockets. "What's up?"

Dad stares at me, and then he looks at Sawyer.

"Hi, Mr. Demarco," Sawyer says. His voice is calm.

I don't say a word.

Dad looks like he's trying to hold it in. His face is red. But he won't make a scene in a public place. Not in front of potential customers. He doesn't answer Sawyer, which feels kind of jerkish to me. Instead, he looks back at me and says, "Tree research. Is that the same as chess club?"

"Dad—" I say.

"Don't bother," he says, and I'm a little freaked out that his voice is so quiet. "Both of you, it's time to go. Julia, you're coming with me. Trey, come on. You take the truck."

"No, sorry, Dad. I'm still working—" Trey begins.

"You'll get home in ten minutes or you're grounded too, like this one."

"Dad, I'm eighteen," Trey says. "I'm graduating from high school in two and a half months." He sits back down. "You can't ground me."

"Watch me."

"No, you watch *me*. Watch me sit here and do my homework like an excellent student. What the heck is wrong with you? I'll be home when I'm finished with it, and I'll get a good grade like I always do, and then I'll go to work for you and do a good job there, too. But right now, I'll sit with Sawyer Angotti if I feel like it, so don't even go there. This stupid rivalry ends with your generation. It doesn't exist in mine."

Dad's face twitches. He gives Trey a long, hard look

that scares the crap out of me, and then he looks at me. "Come on, Julia."

I stand there. And my face is hot, and I feel like yelling, and my stomach hurts.

"Julia," my father says again, his voice ending on a strained note, and I can tell he's about to blow a gasket.

I press my lips together and swallow hard. I shake my head. And I don't move. We stare at each other for the longest five seconds of my life. And then Trey says, "Jules, go with Dad."

I glance at him and frown, but his face is set. I look at Sawyer, and he nods in agreement with Trey.

And I'm like, what the heck? I can't even think clearly. I feel like a total baby. I know I'm going to get reamed the whole way home. And I have a life too—why should I have to go with him?

"Julia!" Dad barks, and now people around us are looking, which I'm sure Dad will blame me for later.

"Fine." I throw the meatball truck keys at Trey's face, grab my backpack and coat, trying to shove my arm through the hole but my stupid cast keeps catching on it. When I give up and move around the table, Dad tries to take my arm. I yank it away from him and run down the steps, leaving Dad following me, and Trey and Sawyer standing there watching over the loft railing. I can't even look at them because I don't want them to see me cry.

• • •

We get into Dad's car, and I'm immediately aware of how seldom I ride anywhere with him. I can probably count the number of times on my fingers. He hardly ever goes out, and when he does, my mom almost always drives.

He leans forward, squinting at the windshield and muttering under his breath as he eases out of the parking space. And for a split second, his mannerisms are so familiar. With a chill down my spine, I realize he reminds me of *me*, trying to drive when I had a vision clogging my windows and mirrors. I watch him in horror. Could it be?

And then he starts in on me. "I don't know what to do with you," he says. "You lie to us about everything. I told you that you weren't allowed to talk to that one."

"Will you stop calling him that? Sheesh, Dad."

"Don't talk when I'm talking!" he roars, his booming voice taking over. "You need to go back to respecting me!"

"You mean being scared of you?"

"Dammit, Julia!" He slams his hand into the steering wheel and for a second I'm scared he's going to drive us off the road. He comes to a hard stop at a light and I'm tempted to just jump out, but that would only prolong this and make it all worse.

I sit there, silent, so he can talk more. Yell more. Like a big hypocrite, he hollers about trust, trust, trust, until I want to throw up, because he has never trusted me, and I no longer trust him. I close my eyes and rest my pounding head on the window. And he goes on and on about what a bad child I am.

And the truth is he's right about the things I did. I lied to him and Mom. I saw Sawyer when I wasn't supposed to. I faked some school projects so we could find time to work on saving some lives. But as long as my parents are being overprotective nutcases, I will have to continue disobeying them, I guess. Because I'm not able to let people die when I can stop it from happening.

Now, shall I try and explain that to Dad?

We pull into the parking lot behind the restaurant. I get out without a word and close the door. It seems like he's done yelling. I stopped paying attention. But before we walk into our apartment door, he says, "I'll talk to your mother about what your punishment will be. Be back down for work in five minutes."

And I look at him. "You're not even going to let me say anything?"

His jaw is set. "What do you want to say that I don't already know? That you're pregnant, too?"

I almost laugh, because he just can't let that idea go, but it also makes me furious because he thinks he knows me, and he thinks I'm out there banging people left and right, and he's just so wrong and that's so not me in any way, and it hurts. "Three things, Dad," I say, winding up. "I want to say three things."

He folds his arms and waits like he's doing me a big favor.

I plunge into the rage headfirst. "One," I say, "I'm not pregnant. I'm not sure why you constantly think I am, but I am not sexually active, so you can just knock it off with that." I can't look at him. "Two, I know about your affair, so it's kind of hard to take you seriously on this whole trust thing. And three?" I forgot what three was. And then I remember. "Three. Find yourself another slave. I quit." And before I can allow the shock on his face to poke into my conscience and make me feel bad, I turn on the wet cement step, open the door, and run up the stairs and into my room.

Twenty-Six

Trey knocks on my bedroom door ten minutes later. "It's me," he says.

"Come on in."

He stands there. "You okay?"

"Yeah, but I'm in deep shit. You're home early."

"Sawyer was worried Dad was going to hit you or something. I told him Dad has never done that, but Sawyer was pretty jittery. I think he feels bad we told you to go with Dad."

"Yeah, what the hell was that?"

"Sorry. I suggested it because I figured it might save you a little grief in the end."

"Well, it didn't."

"We're not at the end yet."

"Let me know when we get there, will ya?"

He laughs softly. "I will once I take my metaphorical beating. He's pretty pissed at me."

I don't say anything. All I can think about is Dad and his stupid affair, and how Trey and Rowan don't know, and I don't know if I should tell them. And I wonder if Dad will kill himself now that he knows I know.

It's the constant question. And then I worry that Dad's going to think Mom told me and be mad at her. I flop down on my bed, finally beginning to realize the scope of what I've done. "I quit," I say.

Trey looks at me like he didn't hear me.

I answer his look. "I quit. My job, I mean. I told Dad I quit."

"Holy shit."

"I know."

"What did he say?"

"I didn't really give him time to answer. He yelled the whole way home." I sigh deeply. "At least now I can work with Sawyer more. If Dad doesn't chain me to the house."

Just then we hear pounding up the stairs. It's not our parents. Three seconds later the bedroom door flies open and Rowan is standing there in her work clothes, bug-eyed. She looks from me to Trey to me again. "What the heck?" she asks. "Dad's on a rampage. Sorry I couldn't warn you in time. I didn't know he'd left until later."

Trey explains. "Rowan texted me that Dad was on his way, but by the time I got it he was already coming up the library loft steps." He looks at Rowan. "Who's working?"

"Dad's in the kitchen. Mom and I are in the dining room. Aunt Mary's up front." She looks at me, her face showing hurt for the first time. "How could you quit? I'm leaving Sunday. Now who's going to cover for me?"

I shake my head. "I'm sorry, Ro. It all happened really fast. Dad went nuts and I just lost it, I guess."

"He's superpissed at you, too, Trey. What did you do?"

Trey rolls his eyes. "I think I humiliated him in front of an Angotti. He told me to go home. I said no. He tried to ground me." Trey laughs bitterly. "He's really losing it. He can't get a handle on that stupid rivalry. Okay, so somebody stole your recipe. Get over it. Make up a new, better recipe."

I bite my lip and look at the floor. I know it's more complicated than that. And I'm starting to wonder if there's even more shit going on with Dad. But as mad as I am about the way he's treating me, I don't think I should say anything, especially about the affair. I've made enough messes for now.

Rowan looks at her phone. "I gotta get back down there," she mutters.

"Hey, Rowan?" I say as she turns to leave.

"What." She's still upset with me.

"They'll figure something out. I'll help them if they need me. If Dad'll let me. They can get Nick or Casey or hire somebody else—they're business owners. Stuff like this happens. But I'm still sorry for letting you down."

She scowls. "It's fine. I don't actually blame you." She pauses once more. "Dad told Mom that you're not pregnant. I take it he accused you of that again."

I nod.

"Well, I understand why you'd quit."

"Thanks."

"What did any of us ever do to make Dad not trust us? I don't get it." She disappears, nimbly zigzagging through the cluttered hallway, and then we hear her feet on the steps once more.

Trey stands up. "I should go down too."

I look up at him. "Everything's such a mess."

He nods. "You should call Sawyer. He was figuring stuff out, remember?"

I'd forgotten. "Yeah, okay," I say.

When he leaves, I pull out my phone.

Twenty-Seven

Sawyer's working and can't talk. We make a plan to meet at the coffee shop again before school. I hang around feeling useless, getting all my homework done in record time, making a veggie omelet for dinner, and getting on the computer to research more schools since that's all I know to do to help Sawyer.

When I've exhausted everything I can think of, I sit down in the living room chair and watch TV. Local Chicago news pops on and I watch it idly. There's something about the food truck festival this weekend, so I pay attention, wondering if Dad signed us up. And then I remember I don't work at Demarco's Pizzeria anymore, and I feel really lonely all of a sudden.

When the segment is over I mute it and stare at the

screen, thinking about how I've messed everything up. My eyes focus on the TV when there's a piece on the University of Chicago, which is where Trey once thought about going until he found out how expensive it is. A reporter stands on the grounds, talking about who knows what, and then the headline pops up. "Vandalism over Spring Break." The camera pans wide and some of the campus is visible, and then my eyes open wide. I lunge for the remote and hit the record button, begging it to get the whole segment. Then I fumble for my phone and call Sawyer.

"Hey," he says.

"Where are you?"

"I'm—"

"Come over. Right now. Can you?"

"I, um, are you kidding me?"

"No. I think I found the school. I have it on my DVR. It's not a high school, Sawyer—it's the University of Chicago!"

"The—okay, but what about your parents?"

"They won't be upstairs before eleven. Come!"

"I'm—I'm turning around. I'm five minutes away. Meet me at the door to your apartment."

"Awesome." I hang up and run to the bathroom to make sure I look okay. And then I go back to the TV and rewind to make sure I actually got what I need. I do—I have the whole show. While I wait, I cue it up so Sawyer can be in and out of here quickly. And then I look around the living room like I'm seeing it for the first time.

"Oh, dear dog," I say. "Oh. Dear dog." It's mortifying. No one has ever seen this. No one.

"Whatever," I mutter. This is more important. And I head downstairs to wait.

Sawyer comes out of nowhere, a sudden face in the door's window. I open it quietly and wave him inside.

"Two things," I whisper as we creep up the stairs. "We have to hurry. And . . . my dad is a hoarder. I'm not sure if you knew that. It's a train wreck in here, I'm just warning you, and I'm really embarrassed, but I want you to know the rest of us don't live like that. It's part of his . . . illness."

He nods. "It's okay," he says. "I knew. You mentioned it in the hospital."

We weave through the apartment, Sawyer pretending like it's the most normal thing in the world to have piles of Christmas lights and bulbs in the dining room but nowhere to put a tree.

In the living room I grab the remote. "Watch," I say. "About a minute in, the camera pans and there are buildings with ivy and a whole row of those trees along a street." I turn on the sound for the first time and hit play. And the segment runs. "Say stop if you need me to," I say. "Can you even see it, or is it the vision?"

"No," he says. "I can see it." Sawyer stands there, coat

still on, and watches. The reporter is talking about recent vandalism—graffiti painted around campus. The students are on spring break this week. She's talking about having time to clean up before school is in session again. And then she says something about the beautiful campus's botanical gardens and redbud trees that are just about to burst into bloom. The camera pans, and Sawyer leans forward, staring, straining as if that'll make the camera go where he wants it to go.

"Stop," he says.

I press pause.

"That's it," he says. He stares at it, taking it all in. "This is it. It's one of those buildings for sure—look at the ivy. These are the right kinds of trees. The snow is almost gone." He looks at me. "And the road. You're a genius. How did you know?"

"By your description. And because of the spring break headline. Is there graffiti on the building in your vision?"

"No. They must have it cleaned off by the time this happens." He rubs his eyes. "I can't believe it. You figured it out. I never thought we'd get it." He turns to me and pulls me into a hug, which feels superawkward here in my house, but I'm not complaining.

Still, the risk is large and I pull away. "Let's get you out of here. We'll figure out what to do in the morning."

He nods and we're snaking back down the steps when the door at the bottom rattles and opens.

Twenty-Eight

Thankfully, it's Trey. He startles when he sees Sawyer in our house, but he recovers quickly and holds a hand up in warning. He turns to look behind him, and I can hear him talking to someone outside. Sawyer and I stand so still I don't even think we're breathing.

"Okay, good night, Tony," Trey calls. He comes inside like nothing's up, then presses his back against the door. "I'm going to murder you both," he says.

Sawyer and I nod.

After a minute, Trey opens the door a crack and looks out. "Okay, get the hell out of here," he says to Sawyer.

Without a word, Sawyer makes a break for it, and Trey scoots me up the stairs.

"What the—" he starts, and he's so stunned he can't even finish.

"I'll show you," I say. "Come on."

He follows me and I show him everything. When he's done watching it, he looks at me. "It's not a high school."

"Not a high school."

"You figured it out by accidentally watching the news."

I nod. "I do watch the news on occasion," I say in my defense. "But I didn't have much time back when I had a job."

He laughs. "Oh, Jules . . . your job misses you."

"Did Dad yell at you?"

"Of course. He also suggested that since I'm eighteen I might want to consider moving out and feeding my own mouth."

"He—he did? He really said that?"

"Yes."

My stomach twists. "Are you going to?"

"I—no, not this time. But if he doesn't stop, I might."

This scares the hell out of me. "But where would you go?"

He looks at me. "Aw. Don't worry. I'm not going anywhere." He punches me in the arm. "Do you think I'd leave you and Rowan here? Come on. Not until I go to college in the fall. And even then, I might have to commute." He pinches and rubs his fingers together. "Money.

Though now I'm starting to rethink things again. I need to decide soon."

He goes into his room, and all I can do is think, *Don't leave me here with them!*

Later, Rowan comes in, and I can hear Mom moving around the kitchen. I'm not quite sure what will happen next, but Trey and Ro and I are all planning on going to the coffee shop to meet Sawyer like this morning. The three of us sit around my bedroom, talking quietly. And it occurs to me that the reason we're so close is that the weirdness gene maybe skipped a generation, and we all get along because it's the only way to survive.

Rowan tells us about her trip and gives us all of her flight information, Charlie's address, his phone number, and his parents' numbers too. And even though I feel kind of odd about letting her go and not telling Mom, I feel very good about where she is going to be now that I've seen Charlie and his mom and their non-hoardy, non-tense house. And besides, I couldn't possibly stop her from going.

We hear Dad lumbering around and I make Trey stay in our room even though he's falling asleep. I don't want to face Dad. But he doesn't come in. We hear their bedroom door close like it's the door to a crypt, and we know he's down for the count. Whether it's just for the night or for a few days, no one ever knows. But we think this latest problem will put him in the sack until Rowan leaves.

And then Mom knocks.

She looks at us all—Rowan on her bed, Trey on the foot of mine, and me on the floor in between, and she gets this melancholy look on her face. I think she's going to say something, or yell at me, or tell me what my new punishment is, but all she does is stand there looking at us, like she didn't realize we were all so grown up. She massages her weary eyes. And then she says, "I am so glad you have each other."

"Aww, Mommy," Rowan says, and gets up off her bed to hug her.

Trey says, "You have us too, Mom."

And I just watch her grow old before my eyes, and I smile at her and hope she knows I love her.

If she has a punishment for me, she doesn't issue it.

Friday morning rolls around quickly. It's the last day of school before spring break, and I half expect Dad to be standing outside our room, waiting to catch us going to school early, but he's not there. We three leave by six and sit at the same table we sat at yesterday, but Sawyer doesn't come. After a while I call him, wondering if he slept through his alarm, but he doesn't answer.

We hang out, unable to do anything without computers

or smartphones, and finally we just go to school, not sure what's going on.

Sawyer is not by my locker. He's not in school. There's no sign of him. And I'm worried. By lunch, I've tried calling him three times, and he doesn't answer.

"I'm freaking out a little," I say in fifth hour with Trey. "We should have gone to look for him at lunch."

"Where the hell would we look?"

"We could at least see if his car is home."

Trey shrugs. "He's probably got the flu or something."

"He looked fine last night."

"Maybe he's skipping. Heading over to University of Chicago to see what he can find out."

"Why wouldn't he answer the phone, then?"

"That . . . I don't know. Okay. We'll drive by after."

The warming trend has continued throughout the day, and there are dirty puddles filling potholes everywhere. I try Sawyer's phone once more after school as Trey abandons a ride from his doucheball friend Carter again and the three of us climb into the meatball truck. And this time Sawyer answers.

"Hey," he says.

I pause and hop back outside the truck so I can have some privacy. "Hey, are you okay?"

His voice is quiet. "So, remember back when my dad called your dad after you stopped by our restaurant?"

My eyes fly open. I look at Trey and Rowan, who are peering out the windshield at me. "Yeah."

"I'm guessing you don't know that your dad returned the favor last night."

I bow my head and press it against the truck. "Oh, God."

"The proprietors were not amused."

"What happened? Where are you?"

"I'm pulling into the school parking lot now. You got room in that ball truck for one more?"

"Hell yes," I say. "We'll make room. We're going to drop Rowan off and head to the university. Trey and I told Dad about the food truck festival this weekend, so he wants us to—" Sawyer pulls up next to us and parks the car, and I just end the call rather than standing there next to him wasting phone minutes. He opens the door, gets out, and slowly turns to face me.

His left eye is swollen, black and purple.

He eases out of the car like he's in pain.

Trey and Rowan burst out of the truck when they see him, and all I can do is stare. "Holy shit."

"Nice, right?"

I go to him. And nobody has to ask what happened.

"Your grandfather didn't seem to care about hiding it this time," I say.

Sawyer shifts his gaze like he doesn't want to talk about it. "It wasn't my grandfather. Let's just get out of here."

Twenty-Nine

We leave his car in the school parking lot—it's safer in case his parents go looking for him, he says. And we drop Rowan off. She knows she's got to stay the model obedient child for a few more days, so she doesn't even pout about it.

Trey drives and we go straight to the University of Chicago. We find the building we need, park the balls in a nearly empty parking lot, and wander the grounds until we find a whole huge section with mostly old buildings—Trey says it's the main quadrangle.

Sawyer walks slower than usual, so we let him take the lead. He talks us through the vision—as much of it as he can.

"I only see one gunman in the outdoor scene—the

short, slight one. I don't know where the other guy is. He's bigger and blond. Maybe he's there next to the smaller one and I just don't see him because he's not in the shot, I'm not sure. So if this is the right sidewalk," he says, pointing to the one we're on, "he walks in this direction, I think."

"Do you know which building it happens in? Can you tell?" I try to sound easygoing. Sawyer doesn't need anybody else harassing him, especially me.

"I don't know."

Trey points. "Look, there's some graffiti. Those two guys are trying to remove it from the stone."

Sawyer and I follow his finger. "I'll go talk to them," Sawyer says.

Trey and I exchange a look and stay back as Sawyer approaches the two painters in front of an old, ivy-covered building. He talks to the guys for a minute and returns to us.

"The vandals were some haters writing slurs at one of the college equal rights groups or something," Sawyer says. "They didn't really know." He frowns, gazing over the grounds, and starts walking through the campus, lost in thought.

Trey and I follow, acting casual when security drives by in their carts. I look at the trees. Definitely budding, and with the warming trend happening, they'll be growing quickly, changing daily.

Sawyer stops, closes his eyes, and massages his eyelids, deep in thought. He covers his ears, then looks up and all around. He walks a few paces up a path between a road and a building and looks all around again. He frowns and mutters something.

"What are you looking for?" I venture.

"The little stop sign. I haven't seen it. It should be here . . . somewhere." He rubs his temples. "The vision is in all the windows. Fucking gunshots won't stop. I can't even think."

Trey and I start looking for the stop sign too.

"It should be there," Sawyer says. "I guess I have the wrong building." He emits a heavy sigh and runs a hand through his hair, gripping it in frustration. "But everything else is right. That building with the ivy," he says, pointing to a gorgeous old building on one side of the quad near where we stand. "The redbud trees. The sidewalk. And suddenly now, believe it or not, the noise and everything stopped. I can't seem to conjure up the vision at all—not in any windows or signs or anything."

"It's because you're doing something right," I murmur, hoping he can find some encouragement in it, but knowing how helpless he must feel.

Trey walks in the direction of where Sawyer pointed. "Maybe we're just on the wrong side of the building," he says over his shoulder. "I'll run around to see if it looks the same from the other side." He starts jogging down the path. I go over to Sawyer.

"Is there anything I can do?" I ask.

There's a distant look in his eyes that's not due to the punch he took to the face, but he focuses in on me and relaxes into a half smile for a moment. He reaches one arm around my neck and pulls me close, kisses the top of my head. "Just don't leave me."

As we stand there together, two girls and a guy all dressed in black pass by us silently, and I think it must be sad to be stuck at school during spring break. And then I think about me going to college someday, and wonder if I'll ever want to go home. Only if Trey and Ro are there too.

Sawyer's arm tightens on my shoulders and his whole body tenses. He puts his lips to my ear and whispers, "I think that's them."

I turn my head and look at their backs. One girl has dark brown hair in a ponytail. The other has short blond hair, a pixie cut. The guy has blond hair too. He's wearing a black knit cap. My heart races, but I'm confused. "I thought you said there were two guys?" I say in a soft voice.

"Come on," he says, and we start to follow leisurely behind them. "I thought they were guys, but I never see their faces and they're wearing black. The guy I see with the gun in the classroom is slight and short. It's that girl, the one with the ponytail."

I bite my lip. Has Sawyer started losing it?

"In the vision she's wearing a knit cap and her jacket collar is up. I'm guessing her hair is tucked into the cap. That's her, I'm sure of it."

"But, Sawyer," I say, "school shooters are never girls."

"Don't be sexist," he says, and I actually hear a little bit of the old, nonstressed Sawyer teasing in his voice, and I know he's sure we just stumbled on a big clue. But he turns serious again as we follow, trying not to look like we're trailing them.

Trey is standing at a crossroads, looking at the ground. The three in black pass him, and the girl with the ponytail gives him a long stare, long enough for Sawyer and me to get a good look at her profile before they continue walking.

"I'm going to follow them," Sawyer says. "I'll meet you back here."

I almost protest, but then I notice the expression on Trey's face. I nod instead. "Be careful." And he continues on without me. I make a beeline to where Trey is standing.

I squint as I approach. "What's wrong?" When I'm close enough to whisper, I tell him, "Sawyer thinks those people are the shooters."

"No way." Trey looks startled and cranes his neck to get a better glimpse. I look down at the ground next to where he's standing. And there's the stop sign that's missing, lying in the grass, a fresh black dirt hole near the base of it. But it's no longer a stop sign. Underneath the word "STOP" is another word in black spray paint.

"'Stop fags,'" I say, reading it, and the anger wells up inside me. I press my lips together and blink back the gritty tears that spring to my eyes. "Wow, the haters are so clever these days."

"Aren't they?" Trey murmurs. "At least we found the stop sign." He tries to shrug off the slur but I know better. I know it hurts him. Then he points to a little blue flag stuck in the ground next to the hole. "Looks like it's flagged to be replaced. I'm sure they'll have it up before school starts again."

"Well, that'll satisfy the evidence in the vision. I think that means the crime scene is somewhere near this building. We'll have to ask Sawyer." Trey and I both look at the sprawling structure, several stories high, with spires and gargoyles adorning it and green ivy creeping up its walls. Trey takes pictures with his phone. I count windows, trying to figure out how many rooms are in there, but it's impossible to tell.

Trey shakes his head a little and looks at me, then looks back at the enormous buildings around us. "Somehow this seems just a little harder than stopping a snowplow," he says.

Thirty

Sawyer comes back after a few minutes. We show him the stop sign and the structure Trey and I guess to be the gorgeous, ivy-colored building in Sawyer's vision where the shooting will take place. Sawyer cocks his head and looks at it through narrowed eyes, taking in the turrets and spires. He glances beyond it, and then he turns to peer along the stretch of buildings the other way. "I don't know. I think it's this one," he says, pointing to Cobb Hall, but he doesn't sound very sure.

"What happened to the shooters?" I ask, making sure nobody else is in earshot.

"They went to the parking lot, got in a car, and took off. I got the car info and license number. Not that it'll do us any good."

"Don't you think we should call the police?" Trey asks. "I think we have to. Isn't it the law or something?"

"Come on, Trey," I say. "We went through this last time. They're going to ask how we know. And then what?"

He's quiet for a second. "Why can't we leave an anonymous tip?"

I think about that. "Okay, that's not a bad idea. Is there a way to do that?"

He shrugs. "Easy enough to find out with Sawyer's phone."

Sawyer is already looking it up. "Yeah, there's an anonymous text line called TXT2TIP. It doesn't give the cops your number."

"So . . . we just say we think somebody has plans to shoot down a bunch of students sometime in the near future?" I think about it for a minute. "I suppose it would be better than nothing."

"Yeah, I guess." Sawyer looks up. "You think I should do it?"

We look at each other and nod. "We need all the help we can get," Trey says. "It would make me feel a lot better about everything."

"Me too," Sawyer says. "Okay, here goes nothing. I sure hope this isn't a trick." His fingers fly over the screen. He stops, reads what he has, and shows it to us.

"That looks good," I say. Trey nods in agreement.

Sawyer takes a breath and lets it out. He presses send. And now the police know there might be a shooting in the near future near Cobb Hall.

There's not much else we can do. We try to peer into windows on the first floor, but none of the ones we can see into look anything like what Sawyer described. We try the doors to the building all the way around, but they're locked.

"You know," I say after we come full circle around the buildings, "we might not want to be seen here. We look kind of suspicious since there aren't very many students. Especially with the graffiti stuff that was happening, and now that the police have our tip . . . I mean, they could be on their way over. Maybe we should get out of here."

Absently, Sawyer touches his puffy eye. "Yeah, that's cool, but how are we going to monitor things to figure out timing? The buds on the trees are near where they're supposed to be. The ivy is . . . well, it's hard to tell if it's the same as in the vision. I don't think ivy changes much from day to day. The new stop sign will be up soon, I'm sure. But maybe there are other stop signs. And the vision doesn't actually show the shooters walking into the building by the stop sign—they're just walking near it. So I don't know." He looks around and we all start heading toward the meatball truck. "How are we supposed to know when it's going to happen?"

Trey shrugs. "All we know is that it isn't happening tonight. And that's the best we can do."

We stop by the food truck festival grounds to check it out like Dad's expecting Trey to do. Trey takes care of booking a spot tomorrow for the meatball truck, and finally we're on our way back home to Melrose Park. We don't say much, but we're all wondering. What day? What time? What building? What room? And I remember the way it was with the crash. Everything pointed to Valentine's Day, but at the last minute I realized it was happening the night before. It was all about observation, noticing the littlest things in the vision, that made the difference. It's unbelievably frustrating that I can't see this thing myself.

"How are the visions?" I ask. It's dark now, and we're out of the city, heading back to school. Trey's driving, I'm in the middle seat. Sawyer's by the window, staring out, tapping out the sound of eleven gunshots on his thigh.

"They come and go." He winces and closes his eyes, and his fingers stop tapping.

"Were you able to decipher any words from that whiteboard once you did a close-up?"

"No."

I look at my lap, cringe, and ask another question. "In

the vision, when you see the shot of the building, is there any particular part of the building that seems to be, like, the focus of the scene?"

He's quiet. Trey glances at Sawyer and then at me. I shrug. He frowns and looks back at the road.

"Yeah," Sawyer says after I've already given up on him. He shifts and stares out the window, and I realize he's looking into the side mirror of the truck. "I mean, not any specific window, but there's a section of what I think is Cobb Hall that gets a close-up."

Without a word, Trey slips his phone from his pocket and hands it to me. I look at him, puzzled, but then remember he took pictures of the building. I go through them until I find a shot of Cobb Hall. I touch Sawyer's arm. "Which part?"

He startles and looks at Trey's phone for a long moment. And then he looks at me. "I can't see the photo," he says.

We stop talking.

Trey pulls the truck into the school parking lot. "Jules, I think you should drive Sawyer home. I'll take this ball bus home and pick you up from Angotti's back parking lot on my first delivery. That'll give you two a little chance to . . . do . . . whatever it is you do when you're alone."

Sawyer doesn't argue, and he and I get out. I wave my thanks to Trey as he takes off again.

We stand face-to-face in the warm, wet air as everything around us melts. I look up into Sawyer's eyes, and he cringes and looks away. "Dammit."

"What is it?" I ask.

He doesn't look at me. "It's in your eyes," he says. "The vision. It's playing in your eyes."

It makes my stomach hurt. I close my eyes, reach up to touch his face, turn his chin back toward me. "Better?"

I feel his breath on my face a split second before his lips touch mine. A thrill runs through me, from my toes up to my throat and ending in a low moan. Sawyer sucks in a breath and kisses me hard, his hands sliding around my neck, under my hair. I lean back against the car door and he presses against me, setting me on fire.

My fingers explore his chest inside his jacket and he flinches once, just barely, just enough to remind me that his father beat the shit out of him last night. I lighten my touch and slide my good arm around his back, pulling him close, chest against chest, legs clenching legs, wishing I could pull his entire body into mine. Wishing I could fix him.

His lips find my neck and I can't think straight. I reach up and slide my fingers through his hair, whisper his name in his ear. His hot breath rakes over my collarbone and his fingers tremble at my shoulder, his other hand sliding down my side and finding the hollow of my back, and then our lips are together once more, softer, gentler, and we're breathing hard.

Sawyer reaches around me for the handle of the door to the backseat, fumbles with it, and then lets it go. "No," he says like he's reprimanding himself. And then, after a deep breath, "No," again. And then he lets the breath go, his cheek against mine and his sigh in my ear. "Jules Demarco," he says, "you scare the hell out of me."

I smile against his earlobe. "I know," I say.

Truth is, he scares the hell out of me, too.

Thirty-One

Saturday dawns clear, sunny, and unseason-
ably warm, and all I can think about is that we're running
out of time and there's nothing I can do. I have no job
for the first Saturday in years and I don't know how to
occupy my time. I hawk over the weather report, put on
my wellies, and sneak out for a walk, studying tree buds
and pining for Sawyer, closing my eyes as I slosh through
puddles in the elementary school playground nearby,
remembering the melty feeling I get when he touches me.
But every time my mind goes there, reality slams me in the
face and I remember all the shit we're in.

And I think it's so ironic that as grounded as I supposedly am right now, I have never felt freer to wander around
and not tell anybody where I am. After I test out all the

swings, I start walking, trying to figure out what we have to do. What I have to do to solve this mystery, to finish the puzzle. Because it still feels like it's my fault—or at least my family's fault for passing down the crazy gene—and I can't *not* take responsibility for it.

By the time I've walked an hour, I realize I'm not far from the Humane Society. I hesitate at the door and go inside, look around, but I don't see Sawyer. The employees are busy with adoptions, so I wander into the dog room and look at all of them, some begging for love, others having given up, still others faking it, pretending they don't need anybody. And I see myself in all those dogs.

Five weird thoughts I've had in my life that I would never admit to having:
1. Um, *that* one
2. That I'm not really me, but I'm sort of just floating above myself watching my body do things
3. That there's something really stable and comforting about hoarding
4. That there's probably an opposite me some- where in a parallel universe doing everything right, and my job on earth is to make her look good by messing everything up
5. That monster spray secretly invites more

     monsters to hide under the bed rather than
     repels them

And while I'm standing there thinking weird thoughts and watching this sweet-looking boxer mutt named Boris, and all the dogs are barking as loud as they can at me and the other people walking through, I feel somebody's gaze boring into my skull. I turn around, and there's Sawyer watching me through the wire-mesh window to the cat room. He's got two black kittens crawling up his sweatshirt, and he's just standing there with this amazingly sweet, kind look on his face. I raise my hand in greeting, and he mouths the words "I love you."

I smile and blush, and weave my way back through the dog room to the lobby and into the cat room, because when a boy with two kittens says he loves you, you do whatever you can to get to him as quickly as possible.

"Hey," I say.

"You found me," he says. He pushes a lock of hair out of my eyes and looks away quickly.

My heart sinks. "Still with the vision in my eyes?"

"Yeah. And all the kitties' eyes too."

"Dude," I mutter, because I never had that. It was never that bad. "How did you get here?"

"Took the bus. I—there's no way I can drive."

I study his face, and even excluding his black eye, he

looks exhausted, and I know he's been keeping the intensity from me. "Sawyer . . . I just don't understand. The times when it got really bad for me were when I had things wrong or the crash was imminent. I just don't know why it's not letting up on you when we're making progress and figuring things out."

And then we both stare at each other. Sawyer says it first. "Maybe we have things wrong."

My heart clutches. "Or maybe it's imminent."

"Shit."

"But it can't be. There are hardly any students on campus. It's spring break."

"Yes, but they've got to come back sometime before classes start Monday."

"You mean, like, today and tomorrow? But who would be using those buildings?"

Sawyer puts the kittens back into their cage and goes to the next cage, pulling a single gray kitten out and handing it to me. He reaches in for another one—a blue tortie, according to the label on the door—and cradles it. "I don't know. But colleges aren't like high schools, are they? I mean, they might have meetings. . . ." He strokes the kitten's back and it mews and tries to bite his thumb. Sawyer readjusts the kitten and gazes down at it, then back at me. "Can you try a search to find out? I've got my laptop with me, but I'm scheduled here until two today."

"Sure. There's got to be Wi-Fi around here somewhere."

"Meet me back here at two?"

I nod. We put the kittens back in their cage and he whispers, "I'm scared."

My spine tingles, and not in a good way. "Me too," I whisper back.

I return at two with no information on any classes meeting this weekend but with a lot more info about U of C and a possible clue to the actual motivation of the shooters. "I think we need to go back to the campus," I say. "Like, now. There has to be a clue. Something."

"What's Trey doing today, working?"

"He and Rowan are at that food truck festival."

Sawyer washes his hands at the sink and says goodbye to the other volunteers and employees. We walk out. "I have to work tonight," he says. And then he frowns and shakes his head. "No, I don't." He pulls out his phone.

He dials and waits. "I'm taking the weekend off," he says in a dull voice, a voice I've never heard.

"Yeah, well, if you make me come in, I'm telling everybody who asks how I got this black eye."

He listens for a second, and then, with no emotion, says, "Fire me, then. I really don't care." He hangs up. "Jesus," he says as we reach the bus stop, his face gray and dead. "I can't deal with this. I really can't."

"I know."

"I mean it, Jules." He rakes his fingers through his hair and cusses under his breath. "My family is a mess. The visions and the gunshots are killing me. I don't have anything . . . left. . . . Shit." He jams his fingers into the corners of his eyes and lets out a shuddering breath, and he turns toward me. I wrap my arms around him, feel his shoulders tremble.

He can't stop. "I mean, what the hell are we supposed to do? We're teenagers. We have no weapons or magical powers here. What are we going to do, Jules? Can you tell me, please? Because we're going to fucking get our heads blown off."

"No, we're not. And today is the day we figure it out. Right now. You and me. And we're not going home until we know what's happening."

He sniffs and clears his throat, like he doesn't want me to see his emotion. But I understand tears, especially about this. Hell, I wish all guys could just cry and not have it be such a big stupid deal. Shed a tear. Be a man. Whatever. But I guess when you live in a house where your father and grandfather beat the crap out of you, maybe you have a different mind-set on that topic.

We get on the bus, trying to figure out where to pick up the transfer that will take us to U of C, and then I open Sawyer's laptop and click on one of the tabs of the web pages I left open. I show Sawyer the history of the school and its beginnings, involving John D. Rockefeller, Marshall Field, and—what I think is the most interesting fact that I didn't know before—the American Baptist Education Society.

I point out the highlights. "So it's this private college with that big Rockefeller Chapel we saw, started by Baptists, yet totally secular from the beginning, I think. The dorms have coed floors, and there's a strong LGBT community."

Sawyer looks puzzled. "I'm not getting why any of this matters to the shooting."

"Rowan said something off the cuff the other day— she wondered what the motivation of the shooters might be. I couldn't stop thinking about it. And if you think about what happened here this week with the graffiti and what the workers told you about a protest over equal rights, and the defaced stop sign that Trey found, it's pretty obvious that somebody's upset with this school or some of the organizations in it, and it has something to do with equality. Since the slur "fag" was used, I'm guessing that it's gay rights that are being protested."

"Okaaay . . . but . . ."

"Hang on," I say, looking up, realizing it's time to transfer.

We change buses and keep reading. Sawyer sets his

phone up to be a Wi-Fi hot spot so I can get online on his computer and he can search for more news on his phone, but it's no use for him. His screen is just a medium for the vision. He leans back and closes his eyes. "I don't know how many more piles of dead bodies I can see before I lose it completely, Jules," he says. "What are we doing wrong?"

I pull up the Wikipedia page for U of C. Normally I don't trust Wikipedia, but this page has a bunch of great photographs, so I browse through them. I locate several of the buildings we saw on the main quadrangle and study them. There's a ton of great detail about the insides of the buildings too—stuff I never expected to find. "Hey," I say, looking over. But Sawyer's eyes are closed, his head nodding against the window. Sleeping. Thank dog. I have a feeling he's going to need it. I go back to scouring headlines.

What I find next stops my breath.

Thirty-Two

I can't help it. I have to wake him up. He blinks and looks around, like he forgot where he was.

"I found something," I say, jiggling my foot impatiently.

"Whoa," he says. "Power nap." The sleep confusion clears, and his face grows concerned. "What is it?"

I turn the computer screen toward him. "Can you see?"

"Yeah. At the moment."

"Cool. Look here, where I researched other local news and protests," I say, clicking over to another tab. "There's that local cult preacher dude who always hangs out by Water Tower Place—you know the one, right? Same guy as always. Anyway, he's been shouting about gays taking over the government again, and he's been ragging on U of C lately because their rights groups have been picketing the guy.

"See this article, 'A Call to Arms Goes Too Far: Free Speech at All Costs'? The dude has been riling up his followers, saying God wants his cult to rid the country of homosexuality, and that the local Chicago universities are the heart of the nation's problem and the leaders of the so-called gay uprising." I look up. "Isn't that insane?"

Sawyer takes it all in. "There's a lot of insanity these days," he mutters. "So you think our shooters are some outsider cult followers of the raging lunatic, coming to campus to . . . do God's will."

"I don't know. But seeing that, plus the graffiti, and the timing of this . . ." The whole idea of it turns my stomach. Who would want to believe in a God like that? If God is not, like, totally in love with *all* the people he created, why would anybody want to believe in him?

Five things a real God should be:

1. Not a hater
2. That about sums it up

After a minute Sawyer nods. "It fits. It's fucking sad, but it fits." He looks at the window for a long minute. He's watching the vision again.

• • •

The bus stops near the college and we walk to campus. There are more people wandering around today than yesterday. The stop sign has been replaced, all the snow piles are melted, and the tree buds are just noticeably more in bloom than yesterday. The grass is sodden and the botanical gardens on the property look pretty bedraggled, but spring is clearly on its way. And the vision clock is ticking.

"How do the buds and ivy compare today?" I ask. We wander around the quad, really looking at each building now that we have a good feel for the lay of the land.

"Really close," Sawyer says.

We go to the other end of the quad to make sure we haven't made any mistakes, and sure enough, there are old, ivy-covered buildings, streets, little stop signs, and sidewalks on this side of things too. Sawyer stops in front of a gorgeous ivy-covered building as a few people come out of the wooden door. He stares at it. I read the words above the door. It's a dormitory—Charles Hitchcock Hall.

After a minute, Sawyer looks all the way down toward Cobb Hall, and then he looks back at the dormitory in front of us. "I wonder if I have the wrong building," he murmurs. "I mean, just because I see the stop sign in the vision doesn't mean it's near the scene of the shooting— they're different frames." He puzzles over it some more. "No. It can't be a dorm room. There's a whiteboard and tables." He shakes his head like he's reprimanding himself. We start walking.

A cute guy wearing funky glasses comes out of the dormitory and sticks a flyer to the building wall. He walks into the quad, heading toward us, handing out more flyers. He looks at us, hesitates, then holds one out and smiles brightly. "GSA is teaming up with the Motet Choir for our final spring food drive and fund-raiser. Meeting in the Hitchcock green room tomorrow night. You should join us."

I reach out and take it, and the guy moves on, heading toward the next dorm. I read the info. Eight o'clock tomorrow night. "GSA. Gay-Straight Alliance," I say, looking up.

Sawyer nods, his voice taking on a trepid tone. "Sounds like this could be the group we're looking for. Plus the time is after sunset, which would make the room naturally darker. Though they'd have lights on, presumably." He frowns.

"I wonder where this green room is."

"Let's go find it."

But the door requires a student ID to unlock it. We wait until someone exits, and Sawyer catches the door before it closes. We walk into Hitchcock Hall and to our right is a large room with brick walls, portraits, couches, and a piano. "Green room?" I guess. I see one of the flyers with "HERE" written over the location in black marker.

"That was easy," Sawyer says. "But it's not the room in the vision." He looks all around, as if hoping to find the items from the scenes. "I mean, I guess they could bring tables and chairs in here, and a whiteboard, but . . ." He looks at the windows and shakes his head. "No. This isn't it. The walls are wrong."

I flop down in a chair, suddenly weary of it all. Nothing is lining up. "How are the visions," I say, barely even a question, just a repetition of every other time.

"Bad."

I lean forward and rest my face in my hands. And for the first time, I feel like we've completely run out of ideas. "And there's nothing new?"

Sawyer sighs sharply and I know I've asked him that once too often. I cringe, not that he can see it, and follow up with a muffled "Sorry" before he says anything. We go back outside to wander aimlessly around campus again.

Before we can figure out what to do next, my cell phone vibrates in my pocket. I look at Sawyer to see if he's screwing around, but he's not. I pull it out and look at the number, and it's Trey. I answer. "What's up?"

"Um, like, where the hell are you?"

I look at my watch, and it's after six. No wonder my stomach is growling. "Sawyer and I took the bus to U of C."

"Mom and Dad are freaking out. They keep calling me

and Rowan and we're trying to run the stinking truck. It's a nightmare. We could actually use your help . . . if you hadn't quit, you know."

I shrug. "Maybe if they buy me a new cell phone they could get ahold of me. You may want to mention that."

"I'm going to tell them that you called me from . . . shit. What do you want me to tell them?"

I look up at Rockefeller Chapel and see a door open, inviting in the spring air. I step inside and see a group of adults wearing choir robes, rehearsing. "Tell them I took a really long walk, looking desperately for a pay phone."

"Whatever. Did you figure anything out?"

I glance at Sawyer, who is sitting on the chapel steps with his head in his hands. "No." I pause, and then I say, "Tell Mom I'm coming to help you. We're only about twenty minutes away."

I hear Rowan utter a muffled swear word in the background. Trey sighs. "Thanks, Jules."

We hang up and I go back outside and hold my hand out to Sawyer. "Hey," I say with fake enthusiasm. "Wanna go run the giant truck o' balls with team Demarco?"

He looks up at me, and despite the situation, a slow grin spreads across his face. "That actually sounds awesome," he says.

Thirty-Three

Trey's eyes light up when he sees us. "Thank the gods," he breathes. "Did you see the line?"

"How could we miss it?"

Rowan's hair is stuck to her forehead with sweat. She grabs a towel and wipes her face, then throws the towel into the dirty bin. "Blown away," she says. "I do not understand why you guys enjoy this truck so much."

I give Sawyer a hasty tour, show him how we do our orders, and set him up filling bread bowls with meatballs and sauce so we can catch up on the backlog. I make him taste everything. "This is excellent," he says, his mouth full.

"Don't be stealing our recipe now," Trey says as he hands an order through the window to a customer.

Sawyer laughs, but he shoots me an anxious look that says, *Does he know about our parents?*

I shake my head and start grating fresh mozzarella like it's going out of style. "No wonder you're blown away. You've got no *mise en place*. You're out of everything."

Trey gives me a scornful look. "Oh, we had everything prepped, I assure you. Again, I refer your gaze to the line out front and ask you to kindly note that it's been like this for four hours."

"Point taken. We'll set you back up. Right, Angotti?"

"Yes, boss," Sawyer says.

I look around and it feels a bit too crowded in here. "Ro, you want to go outside and take orders and hand 'em through to Trey? That way you can go down the line a bit and we can get things moving faster."

"Good call," Trey mutters.

"Gladly," Rowan says. "It's fucking hot in here."

I look at her as she leaves. "When did she start cussing?"

"Mmm. Yeah. That would be today," Trey says.

Sawyer laughs. He works really fast, and once he's caught up with the bread bowl orders, he looks for other things to do. "How can I help?"

I grab bunches of fresh spinach from the cooler and shove them at him. "Rinse, spin, steam two minutes, and rough chop. Got it? Then garlic and onions over in that cooler—you okay chopping onions?"

"Pfft. Of course," he says, like I just insulted him. And I freaking love that he knows everything I'm talking about. I remember my dreams of leaving love notes made of green peppers for him on the cutting board and laugh under my breath.

Once I have the cheese tub filled, I chop tomatoes, and then the orders start getting filled again and the line begins moving.

"Okay," Trey says when we have a good rhythm going. "Catch me up. Are we still looking at Monday or Tuesday for the thing?"

"Don't know," I say. "For a while we were actually thinking tomorrow night, but now we're not sure. Still, Sawyer's visions are so bad he can't drive, and he's seeing them everywhere."

"Tomorrow night."

"Yeah."

"Great."

"At least if it is tomorrow, it'll be over soon," Sawyer says, moving to get onions. He looks in the caddy to see how we dice them and starts in. His knife skills are pretty great, and I'm freaking in love all over again.

"So what's the plan?" Trey asks. "Do we have one?"

"Um . . . ," I say, and I feel really helpless, because we

don't have a plan at all, despite my promise to Sawyer that we'd have one by now.

"I think what we need to do is forget about the classroom," Sawyer says decisively. "And focus on the sidewalk and the shooter guy—girl—walking there. If we stop her, the rest of the plan doesn't come together for them. If she doesn't show up, I bet the other one—or two—abandon the plan."

Trey gets backed up, so Rowan pops in to help with a stack of new orders. "You guys better not die while I'm gone," she says. "I mean it."

"Shit," I say, remembering. "I've got to get you to the airport."

"Yes, you do. You ruin this for me, and I ruin your face, bitch." Rowan smiles sweetly and hands off another order through the window.

"Wow." I glance at Sawyer and he's grinning. He looks at me. "I freaking love you guys. Can I work at your place?"

"Um . . . ," we all say, knowing it was a joke, but I change the subject back to what Sawyer just said. "Anyway, I think you're right, Sawyer—we don't have enough information, so we go with what we know. We know the shooter walks down the sidewalk by Cobb Hall. So we plant ourselves there around sundown in the next few days, or whenever the weather looks like the skies could be dark."

"And that's so easy to predict in Chicago in spring," Trey says. He hands off another order. "Nice, too, that the campus is just around the corner from our house." His sarcasm is evident.

"But we're on spring break, so that's easier."

"But we have jobs."

"Some of us do," pipes Rowan from outside the window.

"This is more important," I say.

"Your face—" Rowan says.

"Shut it," I say. "Inappropriate at this time."

"I love you all," Sawyer says.

"Well, let's just get through this before you go spouting off with your overemotional diatribe," Trey says. "Sheesh. You're even scaring the gays."

"I don't think you understand," Sawyer says, scooping up his diced onions and putting them into the onion bin. "At my place, it's a bunch of old ladies, my parents, my older brothers, who are almost never there, and me. And my cousin Kate—she's cool. But she's in college so she only works a couple shifts a week."

I frown, glancing at Trey, who looks horrified. "That sounds awful," he says.

"It is, trust me."

"And then you also get punched in the face."

There's an awkward pause. Sawyer tries to blow it off. "Yeah. Just one of the many perks of the job."

I shoot Trey a warning glance, but he chooses not to see it. "You know," he says, "once this whole thing is over, we're going to talk about that." He looks at his ticket. "One salad, one balls minus cheese, one heart attack," he calls out. "Come on, step it up back there."

And there's something comforting about Trey being there, knowing he'll be with us tomorrow and the rest of the week too. Once we get Rowan out the door, we're home free.

Thirty-Four

My parents are strangely silent about my being gone all day, probably due to Rowan handing over gobs of money and telling them how I went out to save them when they were blown away. My mother thanks me for helping out, and I respond kindly, coolly, and that's the end of that.

Sawyer and I talk on the phone until he falls asleep. I toss and turn all night, and so does Rowan, making me think she's actually nervous about flying for the first time, all alone.

Sunday morning dawns, and I hear my mother moving around the apartment, getting ready for mass. Rowan has already begged off mass after the long, arduous day on the food truck, and Mom said she could skip today, which was the plan all along. Rowan goes through her duffel bag for the millionth time. By eight thirty, I think I hear Dad moving down the hall, but when Mom leaves, I strain to hear Dad's footsteps on the stairs too and I don't hear them. Rowan looks at me and mouths a cuss word.

I sit up and shrug, hearing his door close again. "Meh. No worries. It's not like he's going to notice us."

Once we're ready, Rowan gets her bag and we sneak out to the pizza delivery car. I have directions printed out and Rowan goes through her purse nervously. "Photo ID, ticket, toiletries," she mutters. She tells me her airline and we head out to the glorious world of O'Hare Airport, a slithering ant farm of a place where even really seasoned drivers choke and get lost. After missing the correct terminal, almost getting plowed over by a bus, and more swearing by the innocent fifteen-year-old I once knew, we finally find the right place, and I do what everybody else seems to do—park any old where I feel like it.

She puts her hand on the door handle and looks at me. "Thanks," she says.

I smile. "Have a blast, okay? And if it's not what you expect, call me. I will come and get you."

She laughs. "You have a few other things on your mind."

"You're my number one," I say. And then I have to

punch her in the arm before things get mushy. "You know what signs to look for inside?"

"Yeah. Don't do anything stupid."

"You either." I pinch her knee, which she hates, and then she's opening her door, slipping out, and she's gone. A second later I roll down the passenger window and yell out, "Call me when you get there!"

She looks over her shoulder and smiles. "I will," she says. She lifts her hand in a wave. And she looks so damn excited it makes me cry.

On the way home I can't get my stomach to settle down. I know our parents are going to freak, and if they find out I drove Rowan to the airport, they'll probably have me arrested or something—I wouldn't put it past them. My dad, anyway. And you know what? I'm trying really freaking hard not to care. Before I head back inside the house I call Sawyer to discuss the plan for the day, which is to get the hell out of here before my parents figure out Rowan is gone.

Inside I can hear the TV, which means Dad is out of his room and hopefully getting ready to open the restaurant rather than sit in the blue TV haze all day with the shades down. They're going to need him down there without Ro and Trey. I feel a twinge in my gut, but I have to ignore it. Today is not the day for that. I slip past the living room and knock lightly on Trey's door.

He opens it and lets me in, closing it behind me.

"You ready?" I whisper. "Mom will be home any minute."

Trey sighs. "Yeah, about that," he says. "I think I need to stay here, for the afternoon at least. You're pretty sure this thing is happening in the evening, right?"

I nod.

"I'll meet you guys out there before dark. I just think I should be here for when they find out about Rowan, you know? So they don't call the cops."

I sit down on his bed and rub my temples. He's right, of course. And he's the best one to handle them.

"Yeah, okay," I say.

"If anything crazy happens, call me. I'll be there as fast as I can."

"Okay," I say again. On an impulse I reach out and hug him around the neck. My cast clunks against his head.

"Ouch. When are you getting that stupid thing off?" he asks, laughing.

"Friday morning. If we all live that long."

"And we have multiple opportunities to die," Trey says. "Death by exploding heads. Er, I meant Dad, not . . . the other." He cringes.

"That was bad."

"I know. Sorry."

I rap on his chest with my knuckles. "We'll be in the quad. I'll call you if anything changes."

His lips press into a wry smile. "Be careful," he says. "It's not worth dying for, okay?"

I nod. And I know. "We're calling the police as soon as we have an idea of what's happening, and when, and where."

I open Trey's door and almost run into my dad. "Oh. Sorry."

He startles too and hits one of the stacks of Christmas tins. Finally, after years of waiting, they come crashing down, making way more noise than something so light-weight should make. I stoop down and help pick them up, putting them back on the precarious pile as best I can with my dad blocking the hallway. I hand the last one to him, not quite looking him in the eye.

"Thank you," he says.

I nod and back into Trey's doorway again so he can get past me.

"And thank you for helping your brother and sister yesterday," he says gruffly. "Mom will add those hours to your final paycheck."

"That's fine."

He doesn't ask me if I want my job back. And I'm too proud to ask for it.

Scary how much like him I am.

Thirty-Five

Dad goes into his bedroom, and I duck into mine, grab my backpack, make sure I have my phone, and scoot out of there. As I descend the stairs, I hear my dad calling for Rowan, and I can't run away fast enough. "Trey Demarco, you are a saint," I mutter under my breath. I owe him big for handling this.

The sky is dark. Occasional giant drops of rain splat on the pavement in front of me, and I wish I'd thought to bring an umbrella. I grab the bus to Sawyer's neighborhood, call him to let him know I'm coming, and just miss a wave of pouring rain. It's only spitting by the time I hop off. And when I look down the street toward Angotti's Trattoria, I see Sawyer walking toward me.

"Okay, so here's what I know," he says in greeting.

"Main shooter girl is holding a Glock 17 Gen4. It holds at least seventeen bullets. She doesn't have an additional magazine on it."

"Hmm," I say. This information means nothing to me, other than the fact that the killer woman can shoot at least seventeen times. Which is more than eleven.

Sawyer grips my hand as the almost empty bus pulls up and he buys two fares. We grab a seat in the back. "Also, I finally managed to figure out a few words on the white-board. Musical terms and composer names." He flashes a triumphant smile.

"How did you manage that?"

"Every time I tried to zoom, the pixels went nuts and I couldn't read anything. But I finally thought to use my mother's reading glasses to magnify the words—she's, like, totally farsighted—and I got these words: Rachmaninoff, Vespers, E A Poe, The Bells."

I frown. "Edgar Allan Poe is a writer, not a musician."

"Right, but I looked up 'The Bells,' which is by Poe, and Sergei Rachmaninoff turned it into a symphony."

I feel a surge of hope for the first time in a long time. "So it's a music classroom, you think?"

"That's what I think."

"So, wait—the victims are not the Gay-Straight Alliance people? It's, like, a regular music class?"

Sawyer's breath comes out heavy, and his face is

strained. "All I know is that the GSA is meeting in the green room, and the room in the vision is a regular music classroom. So the two events don't appear related."

"But that means . . ."

"We've got everything wrong. But at least we know it's probably not going to happen today—there are no classes in session until tomorrow."

I think for a moment. "But the weather is supposed to be sunny tomorrow, and you said it's cloudy and the pavement is wet in the vision."

He shrugs. "Maybe there are sprinklers on the quad. Or maybe it rains when it's not forecasted—wouldn't be the first time."

"True." I look out the window. "So, wait. Why are we going there today, then?"

"To see if we can find the music classrooms and figure out which ones have evening classes. Hopefully the buildings will be open now that students are returning from break." He pulls out a map of the entire main quad, and it's like he's been energized.

"Are you . . . feeling okay?"

He looks at me. "Actually, for once, yeah. The vision calmed down after I figured out the music thing. So I feel like I got something right."

We stop for an early dinner near campus at Five Guys and spend a couple of hours talking everything through.

Sawyer tells me the entire vision one more time, using the map to point out where he thinks things are. I borrow his phone to check the weather, but it still calls for sunny skies tomorrow.

"Question," I say. "In the vision, when you see the, uh, girl," I say, looking around to see if anybody can hear me, "do you see other students around? Like, do you get a broad view of the quad?"

"No other students, no broad view. Just the sky and tree, then the grass and pavement and little stop sign. We zoom in to the building, then out to see the back of the girl's body, and then we're in the classroom."

I look more closely at the map, seeing the individual buildings labeled. "Do you think the music building is in the main quad?"

"That's my guess."

I frown and start googling the names of the buildings around the Snell-Hitchcock Halls. "These are mostly sciencey. Like labs and stuff." I keep going. "Cobb. That's the building with the ivy that we thought the vision was focusing on the other day, right?"

"Yeah." He's got his laptop out and is searching too.

"Here," I say. "Music. It's this one next to Cobb. Goodspeed Hall. Offices, music classrooms, and practice rooms all on the bottom four floors. Practice rooms open seven days a week."

"Sweet." After a minute, Sawyer looks up. "Is Trey coming?"

"Oh, crap," I say. "Yeah. Does he need to? Are you sure it's tomorrow?"

"It's a classroom, Jules. It'll be tomorrow."

"Okay, well, that's probably better timing. . . ." I whip out my phone and call Trey.

He answers and says in a curt voice, "Not now. I'll call you later."

"Oh," I say, but he's already hung up. I look at Sawyer. "He's handling the Rowan thing." I drum my fingers on the table, suddenly nervous about that. She should have called me by now. Hours ago, in fact. I call her cell phone.

"Are you alive?" I almost yell when she answers.

"Shit," she says. "I forgot, I'm sorry, I'm sorry. I figured you knew I made it since Mom's been screaming at me on the phone for the last two hours."

"Yeah, well, I'm not at home. How's it going?"

"Good. I think Trey has them settled down enough not to call the cops, and poor Charlie here is kind of pissed at me for doing this without them knowing."

I hadn't thought of that. "Ack. Do his parents know?"

"Not yet. Hopefully not ever." She hesitates and I hear her talking to someone. "I gotta go, Jules. Love you."

"Love you, too."

"And, Jules?"

"Yeah?"

But she doesn't say anything, and I figure one of us hit a dead spot or she's got to answer another call from our parents. I bite my lip and hang up. And then I look at Sawyer. "I think I'd better head home."

He smiles. "Yeah, you definitely should. Poor Trey." He gathers the wrappers and we get up. "I'm going to go to the campus and see if I can figure out the classroom situation."

I feel terrible leaving him here alone. "Are you sure you're cool with that?"

"Hundred percent."

I glance at my watch. There's a bus in twenty-three minutes. "Okay. Call me whenever you find out anything. And when you're on your way home. And when you get there. And if anything weird happens."

He grins. "I'll call you every five minutes just to let you know I'm still alive."

I grin. "That sounds perfect." I look outside, and it's sprinkling again. The sky is a roiling cauldron of dark, angry clouds. We go outside and I reach up to kiss him, and then we split up, him to campus, me to the bus stop.

As I stand there under the shelter of a nearby over-hang, the rain pelting down, I grip my phone, waiting for it to ring. Waiting to hear from Sawyer. Or Trey. And I think about my parents, and Rowan, and how everything we're doing feels so underhanded, and I kind of don't like myself much these days. It's way too easy to lie. I have an argument with myself, telling me that there's no other way to go about it. That all the superheroes have to lie to hide their true identity, and this is a lot like that.

"Except you're not a superhero," I mutter. "You're a not-quite-seventeen-year-old kid with a contagious mental disorder." I bounce on my toes, waiting for the stupid bus, which is most certainly late. "Come on. Somebody call. I'm anxious." I pause, and then I say, "I'm so anxious I'm talking to myself."

Finally, ten minutes late, the bus pulls up just as the heavens open. I watch the people get off and prepare to make a mad dash for the bus door.

And then I see her getting off the bus.

It's the girl. The girl with the gun.

Thirty-Six

Her black hat is pulled down over her eyes, and she looks like a guy. She's alone. I think. She's wearing dark-wash jeans and a black jacket, and she's gripping a little backpack so hard her knuckles are white. And on the backpack is a button with a picture of a rainbow with a line through it. My heart thunks around in my chest and I almost can't breathe. *So it* is *the GSA they're after?* I'm so confused.

The bus driver inches forward and cranes his neck at me. I shake my head and wave him off. And after a second, I follow the girl. I let her get a few dozen feet ahead of me and inch my phone from my pocket. I dial Sawyer's number, but nothing happens. No signal. I try him again, and then I look at the phone battery. It's not dead. But there's a little notice in the corner in the tiniest print that says "minutes used: 250."

"Shit," I mutter. And then it really hits me. My prepaid minutes are used up. I have no phone. No wonder neither of the boys has called me.

I have no phone.

I look up to make sure the girl is still in sight. At the corner where we'd turn to go to U of C, she stops and waits for traffic. I pretend to look in a shopwindow, and then when the light changes I begin to follow again. And I don't know what I'm going to do. I don't know what she's going to do. For all I know, she's just doing one more stakeout of the campus in preparation for tomorrow. But the way she's gripping that little bag tells me otherwise.

Thankfully, the rain keeps her from looking around. She scurries along, head down, and when we cross a street, she's joined by the blond guy who she was with the other day. They barely say two words to each other, and then they walk together but not very closely. And I realize this is really it.

My hand finds my phone again and I try a few more times in case I'm wrong and the minutes haven't expired, but it's futile. My phone is useless. I want to run ahead, try to find Sawyer, but I don't want them to see me, and I don't want to lose track of them. I follow the two into the quad as the rain stops, the only drops now coming from the trees.

"Where are you?" I mutter. The quad is huge, and there are a lot of buildings. And the campus is alive again with students running through the rain, transporting their suitcases, bags, and backpacks back to their dorms. I want to go toward the hall we determined was the music building, but the two people in black go to the opposite corner of the quad toward the Hitchcock Hall dorm. I strain my eyes looking for Sawyer, but I don't see him anywhere.

My chest is tight. I hear a distant church bell chiming the hour as we near Hitchcock Hall. Eight bells. The two in black stop at the side of the big wooden door and stare at something as people dash in and out of the building. The guy looks panicked for a moment, but the girl shakes her head slightly and says something. I stay by the road, trying to look like I'm waiting for someone, trying to hide that I'm praying my brains out to whoever will listen that Sawyer is okay.

The two stand there whispering for a minute, and then they come back toward me. I freeze, and then I pull a notebook from my backpack and rip a page out. I fumble for a pen and keep my head down as they pass by me, pretending to write things down. And then I walk as fast as I can to the Hitchcock door to see what they were looking at.

It's the Gay-Straight Alliance flyer. But the green room meeting place is crossed out and instead it says, "Moved to Goodspeed 4th Fl!!"

The blood pulses in my ears. That's the music building. And suddenly everything I can remember from Sawyer's vision is coming together and making sense. It's all happening right now, and Sawyer doesn't know. I look at the torn sheet of notebook paper in my hand, write, "Call 911—Goodspeed 4th Fl!" and take off after the shooters at full speed, shoving my paper into the hands of a surprised student as he enters the dorm.

I race across the quad to Goodspeed, splashing through puddles, soaking wet, watching the shooters enter the music hall. When I reach the door I dash up the stairs to the fourth floor, trying to look casual, as others move through the short hallways, some carrying backpacks or musical instrument cases. And I don't even care about the massive deaths right now. All I can think of is that I need to find Sawyer and get him out of here. We're not ready. We can't do this. We need to bail. Just call the cops, get the hell out of the way, and hope for the best.

A few students wander the fourth floor, some of them peering at closed office doors or into classrooms, and I'm guessing they are looking for the same room I am. And then I spy the cute guy with the glasses who handed us the flyer yesterday. He's down the hallway, standing in front of an open door, frowning at his watch. "Come on, people," he says.

He takes a look at my wet clothes and hair. "Now that's

dedication," he says with a grin. "Hey—I remember you. Your boyfriend is inside."

My eyes bug out. "I—he—what?"

His kind eyes crinkle. "Oops. Did I get that wrong? I thought you were holding hands the other day. I'm sorry."

"No, I mean . . . never mind. Thanks." I push past him into the room and look around, spying the two shooters immediately at the front table. Sitting at the table behind them is Sawyer, whose normally olive complexion is alabaster now. He stares at me. I walk in like I don't know him and go to the window.

A minute later, he's next to me. "What happened?" he whispers.

"It's now," I say back.

"No shit. You could have answered your phone!"

"Ran out of minutes. Couldn't call you either. Now what?"

"Ohh," he says. "Crap. I should have thought of that." He glances over his shoulder. "I texted the tip hotline. Can't exactly call."

"We can get out of here. There's time."

Sawyer grips my arm. "No, we can't. It's changing. The vision. Us being here is changing it. Fewer gunshots, fewer bodies. Down to seven. We have to stay and try to stop it."

"But what if the bodies are *us*?"

"Jules," he says, and he grips my wrist. "Remember how it was with you. You have to trust me." There's no time for him to explain—the cute guy clears his throat loudly and announces that it's well past eight. Sawyer gets a text message and responds quickly as we sit down at the table. I question him with my eyes. "Trey," he mouths.

My eyes widen, begging for more information. But Sawyer glances at the shooters and shakes his head. He puts his hands below the table and holds out nine fingers, then one, then one again.

"Oh," I breathe, relieved. *Trey's calling the cops.* Everybody continues to make small talk except for the shooters, who sit there stone-faced.

From the doorway, the cute guy asks the students to finish up their conversations. He looks down the hallway once more and closes the door. "Okay, everybody, settle. Sorry about the last-minute venue change—the green room was too noisy with everybody coming back from break with all their luggage and parents and junk." He looks around the room and grins.

"If you don't know me, I'm Ben Galang, freshman, next year's secretary of the alliance, and this is my first time organizing a charity event, so yeah. Help a guy out, will ya?" He laughs. A few people smile. "Okay, well. Welcome to the choir members, some of whom are already part of the GSA here at UC. It's great to work with you all and to see some new faces." He smiles at somebody on the other side of the room, at Sawyer and me, and at the shooters.

I can't smile back. I don't dare to turn my head to see who else is in here. I'm freaking out. I can't even focus on what this guy Ben is saying. All I can do is stare at the shooters in front of me, stare at the girl's black bag, at the bulge on the blond guy's hip, under his jacket. I glance at Sawyer and he's sweating, watching the glass in the door, and I know from experience that, one, he's watching that vision *very* closely and, two, all I can do is trust him and follow his lead, because he's the only one who knows how this is all going down. And if I mess with it, it could change everything. I dare a quick glance around the room at the faces, all these faces that Sawyer has been seeing for weeks with bullet holes in them, but my mind can't even record them—they are all a blur of one victim's face.

Sawyer's elbow touches mine, and I look at him. He points to the clock above the door. "New scene," he whispers. Does that mean he knows the time this will happen? He points to the table and mimics flipping it. Then he points to the girl and looks at me.

I nod. He scratches his knee and looks at me again. I swallow hard and panic—I don't know what that means. He points to their legs, his fingers shaking, and finally I understand what he's trying to say. I nod again. And then he spreads his hand out on his thigh, five fingers, and before I know it he hides his thumb, and then his first finger, and I realize that he's counting down, and this is happening in two, one . . .

The shooter girl pulls a gun from her little black backpack, stands up, and whirls around, yelling, "All you fags to the back of the room!" The blond guy follows her lead, pulling his gun out and shoving their table out of the way, but at first nobody else in the room moves. Nobody understands what's happening. They're in shock.

It all goes in slow motion. Sawyer and I flip our table, trying to give others something to hide behind. Ben, smile fading, turns to see what the commotion is all about. Sawyer springs forward from his chair, stays low, hops over the table, and tackles the blond guy at the back of the thighs, making his knees crumple. A shot rings out, hitting the ceiling light fixture. The whole row of lights goes out, leaving us in semi-darkness, and that wakes me from my frozen state. I dive from my seat and tackle the girl the same way Sawyer tackled the guy. She loses her balance and lands on my back as two more shots pierce the air and shatter my eardrums, along with a chorus of screams.

"Run!" I yell from under the girl, pulling sound from the depths of my lungs. "Go! Get out! Run!" I hear tables and chairs scraping and crashing, people screaming, almost everyone running for the door as a few more shots ring out.

Sawyer gets on top of the blond guy and starts pounding his wrist, trying to get him to let go of the gun, and it goes off again, but I can't afford to look at what, or who, it hits. I struggle to get the girl off my back, rising quickly to my hands and knees to throw her off balance. I can feel her weight shift, and she teeters, grabbing my hair and yanking it, trying to hold on. I reach deep, finding some other inner strength, and try to buck her off me, digging my cast into the floor like a cane to push me up. The girl's gun hits me in the head as she loses her grip on my hair and falls to the floor.

I scramble aside and turn to look where she is. She kicks me in the face, and I see stars. As she gets to her feet she starts screaming over and over, "Die, you sick fags!"

My cheek throbs. I try to grab her around the ankles, but all I get is her pant leg, which she rips from my grasp, taking parts of my fingernails with it. She stumbles off balance and kicks me again. Awkwardly I reel away from her kick, then try to catch her foot, but instead I trip over a chair and I'm back on the floor once again as she catches herself and stares at me like she hates me. I roll to my stomach and cover my face like a coward because I think this has to be the end for me.

I hear three gunshots and I don't know if anybody's hit. I freeze in place, cringing and crying, figuring she'd be shooting at me, but she isn't. At least I don't think so, anyway. When I dare to look, she's grabbing Ben, who is stoically trying to drag a bloody person out of the room. The shooter girl shoves him, makes him turn around to face her, digs the gun into his forehead, and backs him up against the wall just as Sawyer and the blond guy, rolling on the floor, bump into me. I can hear Sawyer cussing, trying to stand but slipping on a smear of blood, twisting crazily and falling hard. With the momentum, Sawyer manages to extend his arm, slamming it down across the shooter's chest.

The blond guy's gun goes flying. I get to my hands and knees and crawl after it, trying shakily to get to my feet, but the guy grabs me and yanks my legs out from under me, making me land hard next to him. I hoist myself up with my good hand, swing my cast around awkwardly to block his fist, and slam my knee into his groin before he can choke me. He gasps and shrivels up, his face telling me I nailed him just right, and I'm free. But my muscles are in shock and I can't get them to obey me. I roll away, out of his reach, searching desperately for Sawyer.

Sawyer's got blood on his face and he staggers to his knees, crawling around desks and chairs and broken equipment, trying to get to the guy's gun, while I refocus on the girl with the gun to Ben's forehead as she screams in his face, and for the first time I feel like we have failed. I am helpless to save him. I know he's about to die, and there's nothing I can do. "No," I whisper, and I can't even hear the word come out because of the screaming. But Ben is silent, stiff, gun jabbed between his eyes, facing the girl and barely flinching. Something about his bravery gives me the weirdest sense of courage. I grab the edge of a table and stagger to my feet once more.

Then the door bursts open. It hits the wall hard, the glass window shattering and sprinkling shards everywhere. The girl turns her head at the noise, and Ben—the new, desperate leader Ben—slams his fist into her gut and she doubles over. Her gun goes off. And just as Sawyer staggers over to grab the blond guy's gun, I fling myself at the girl and start flailing my arms and legs, feeling like I've got no plan but nothing to lose. I kick the crap out of her arm that holds the gun, and I whack the shit out of her face with my cast, once, twice, three times, until she drops, and I kneel on her fucking head as she screams.

With a ragged breath, I look up at the door, suspecting it was the police who shattered the window within it, but all I see is my brother's startled face, his body leaning against the wall.

"Trey! Thank God!" I shout. And then I watch him sink to the floor, leaving a streak of red on the wall behind him.

Thirty-Seven

"Trey!" I scream again, but I can't let up on the girl. I move my free leg around and step hard on her arm as she screams out in pain, screaming her hatred, calling me a sick fag, calling me an abomination, telling me I belong in hell. Telling me God hates me. Ben comes running to kick the gun away from the girl, and finally, finally, the police come.

It takes them a few minutes to sort out the good guys from the bad, especially with the girl screaming at us. As soon as they've got her, I crawl over a slippery floor to Trey, where another cop is trying to talk to him, telling him to stay awake, telling him help is on the way.

"Back off," the cop says, holding his arm out to push me back. "Give him some room."

"He's my brother," I cry, my voice ragged, and the guy lets me near him again. "Is he breathing?" Blood spurts out from somewhere around his shoulder.

"Yes. What's his name?"

"Trey. Trey Demarco."

Within seconds the paramedics are there, assessing all the injured, and I follow their gazes around the room, suddenly remembering Sawyer again in all of this. Two of the paramedics run to a girl who is lying against the back wall, eyes glazed, holding her side as blood spills from between her fingers, and I don't want to see that, but I can't look away.

On the other side of the room, the blond shooter gets shoved to the floor and handcuffed, and the girl shooter still hollers hate speech as she's being held by two cops. And then there's Ben Galang, glasses knocked off, face bleeding. Ben Galang, who almost surely should be dead, reaching out and helping Sawyer to his feet.

There's one more guy near the door who cries out, trying to scrape himself along the floor, his foot bleeding profusely.

That's it. That's all. Everybody else made it out.

I look at Sawyer as the paramedics take the girl with the stomach wound away first, and then they load Trey onto a stretcher. Sawyer stares back at me, his face as stricken as mine feels. I turn to the paramedics. "He's my brother. Can I go with you?"

The paramedic looks at the cop, who nods. "Just her."

"What hospital?" I ask.

"Down the street—to the UC ER. Let's go." They hoist him up until the wheels click into place.

I check to make sure Sawyer hears it, and he nods. And then, with tears in his eyes, he mouths, "I'm so sorry."

Later, after Trey has been wheeled into the ER, a doctor checks me over. He gets an intern to cut my blood-soaked cast off, and we decide there's no reason to put a new one on since I was getting it off later in the week anyway.

While I'm sitting there, the cops arrive to interview me and the others who have trickled in. I tell them what happened, my voice getting shaky all over again. "We were sitting in chairs," I begin, "and Ben was leading the meeting. The girl and blond guy got up and pulled guns out. My friend Sawyer and I both reacted—the shooters were right in front of us so we saw them. The girl was yelling hate speech against the LGBT students. I dove for the girl's legs to knock her off her feet. Her gun went off a bunch of times . . . I'm not sure how many. I saw that Sawyer had the other guy on the floor." I tell them how the girl got away from me and held the gun to Ben's head, and then how my brother burst in and broke the glass in the door, and how that distracted the girl and Ben punched her and she shot Trey instead.

And when they ask me how I knew to react so quickly, I just look at them. "I don't know," I say. The cops seem satisfied, and they're gone before my parents arrive.

My parents.

Yeah.

Five things I don't want to talk about:

1. Why the heck Trey and I were getting shot at when our little sister was missing
2. Why we were clear on the other side of the city when we were supposed to be grounded
3. How on earth their good son could be with them one hour and shot in the arm the next
4. Why we want to give them so much grief, because first the crash and then Rowan and now this
5. How that Angotti boy fits into all this mess

And all I can think to say in response is "At least I didn't wreck the balls."

They are not amused. But thankfully, they have a lot of other stuff on their minds.

And after the docs get a good look at Trey and fix him up, they tell us we are very lucky, because the bullet passed through the muscle of his arm and didn't hit any bones and barely nicked an artery. And while there may be some nerve damage, he should regain full use after a few months. They're going to keep him here for a couple of days.

Once I get to see that Trey's all right, I wonder where Sawyer is. I leave Mom and Dad in Trey's room and venture out to the waiting room. And there, either stupid or stoic, is the boy I love. The blood on his face is wiped clean, and he has a couple of stitches on his forehead. Sitting next to him are two guys. One I don't recognize, and the other is leaning forward with his face in his hands, and I don't realize who he is until he looks up. It's Ben.

Sawyer stands up fast when he sees me. He looks me all over. "You okay?"

I nod. I have some bruises, a few cuts, but that's it. "You?"

"Fine. How's Trey?"

"Trey's okay," I say, and it's clear by the look on Sawyer's face that he hadn't heard anything yet. "I'm sorry, I thought they'd tell you."

"No."

"Have you heard anything about the others?"

"They're alive," Sawyer says.

Ben glances at Sawyer with a puzzled look. "How do you know?"

"I mean, I guess I don't know," Sawyer says, giving me a look that says he really does. Because the vision changed,

I'm sure, like mine did, right there at the end. "But they were alive when the paramedics took them. So I hope . . ."

Ben stands up and comes over to us. "Hey," he says to me. "I don't know if you remember. I'm Ben Galang—"

"Freshman," I say. "Just voted in as next year's secretary." I smile. "Your first charity event ever."

Ben's face crumbles, and I feel terrible. Because he doesn't know everybody lives. He doesn't know how bad it could have been.

"Shit," I say. "I'm sorry. I'm stupid. I'm just a stupid non-college student who is, um, stupid."

He holds back his emotion, and then he says, "You guys saved our lives."

And you know what's funny in a not-funny way? I almost forgot that part, because I got so wrapped up in the clues that none of the tragedy seems real. And I hate that about me. Sawyer shrugs and says, "We just had the clearest view of what was happening." He looks at me. "Gotta stay on your toes when you run with danger girl's crowd."

I squelch a smile. "You guys want to check on the others? I should get back to my family. See if I can get my parents to stop freaking out."

Sawyer gives me a sympathetic smile, and then we hold each other for a long minute, unable to talk about it all right now, but both of us saying everything we can with a kiss to a forehead and one to the lips.

When his arms stiffen, I turn around, and he lets me go. My mother is there in the doorway. She shakes her head and opens her mouth to speak, and then shakes her head again, like she can't believe my gall. And then she closes her eyes and sighs heavily. "Hello, Sawyer," she says.

"Hi, Mrs. Demarco."

"You're not too badly hurt?"

"No, ma'am."

"Your parents . . ." She looks around.

"They're not here."

She nods, unable to hide her relief. "Well."

"We were just leaving," Sawyer says. He looks at Ben and the other guy, who now rests his hand on Ben's shoulder, and I wonder if he's Ben's boyfriend.

"I'd like to thank your son," Ben says. "He saved my life. He . . ." Ben stops talking.

"Now's not a good time," my mom says. "Tomorrow, when Antonio isn't here. That would be better."

Ben nods. "I'll come by. Thank you."

My mother smiles grimly. "I'm glad you're all okay."

Sawyer and the others file out of the waiting room and go down the hallway to the elevator. I look at my mother, waiting for her to yell at me some more.

And all she says is "Your father told me you know about his affair."

It takes me a second to change gears.

"Yeah," I say. "I do. I told him that."

Her face is pained. "Do the others know? Trey and Rowan?"

"No."

She looks away. And then she says, "Do you know where in New York Rowan is?" Her voice is broken and weak for the first time, and I realize she's trying to hide her tears from me. "That's all she'll tell me."

"Yes. She's safe, Mom."

She puts her hand to her eyes like a shield, a brim for the tears, and she breaks down, unable to hold in her sobs. And I stand there, scared, in shock, watching her cry for the first time, and I don't know what to do because we're not exactly a hugging family, and I don't think she probably wants me to. So I watch her, dumb, cold, as she sobs into her hand. And I hate that. I hate myself for not hugging her. I hate that the Demarcos can yell like crazy but that's the only emotion in our tiny repertoire of feelings that we're allowed to express.

Mom drives, and we ride in silence once Dad gets the clue that I'm not speaking to him no matter what he says to bait me. When we get home, I go straight to my room, the only Demarco kid left, and I have no phone. No way of talking to Trey or Rowan without my dad eavesdropping. No way of calling Sawyer without Dad checking the numbers, because he's so controlling and paranoid. So all I can do is lie on my bed in the dark, alone, and stare at the flashing light that pulses on my wall, thinking about the horrible event that happened today, and wondering why I'm so fucking cold inside.

Thirty-Eight

In the morning I grab my savings money, leave a note for my parents telling them I'll be with Trey all day at the hospital, and head down the stairs. The sky is still cloudy, but it's not raining. I debate taking the delivery car, but that'll just piss my parents off more, so I'll take the bus. I descend the steps and go outside.

"Hey," says a voice.

I whirl around, and there's Sawyer standing next to the back door. "You scared me," I say. "Guess I'm a little gun-shy."

He cringes. "Too soon."

I nod. I don't know what my problem is—I feel like I just finished playing a video game or something, like everything that happened yesterday wasn't real. And I don't know what's wrong with me.

We walk to his car and get in. "Are your visions gone?"

"Completely. It's insane."

I laugh, and he frowns again. "It's not funny."

"I know." On the seat is the newspaper, and on the front page is a picture that looks familiar. I pick it up and open the fold, and stare at the students in the quad outside the door to Goodspeed Hall. In the foreground paramedics are loading somebody into an ambulance, and students' faces are in agony. And then I read about it. The whole story, plus some quotes from witnesses: "Two students—I don't know their names—they, like, tackled the shooters and screamed for us all to run . . . and we did. We left them there and we just ran."

I read that there were two other injured students who managed to make it out and down the elevator, and they directed the police to the right place. And I read about a guy who said, "Some girl ran by me and shoved a note in my hand that said to call 911, so I did. I didn't know her. I'd never seen her before."

I look up and realize we're still sitting in the parking lot, and I can't read any more because tears are streaming down my face. And I look at Sawyer and he's crying too, and he reaches over to me and he holds me and we cry together for a very long time. And it's real now. Suddenly it's really freaking crazy real. *That* happened. And we were sitting right in the middle of it. And Trey could have died.

"You're sure you're not seeing any more visions?" I ask after I've wiped my eyes and we're on the road, heading for the hospital.

"I'm sure. It's gone."

"Thank God. It's really over." But the relief I want to feel isn't coming.

He glances at me. "How did you decide to come back?"

I'm not sure what he's asking at first, but then I realize what he means. "The girl with the gun—she got off the bus I was going to get on, so I followed her. When did you figure it out?"

"I ran into Ben in the quad as he was changing the location. He recognized me from the day before and asked where I lived. I told him I was still in high school and checking out the campus for the weekend, thinking about going there for college. I told him I thought what he was doing was cool. He latched onto that and sort of dragged me with him, but then I realized we were headed for a music classroom. That's when everything came together. I tried calling you but you didn't pick up. . . . I figured you were on the bus asleep or something." He glances over his shoulder as we merge. "I'm sorry about your phone. I never thought about you having it long enough to run out of minutes. I guess I figured your parents would get you a new phone when you started doing deliveries again."

"They made me take Rowan's on the few times I did deliveries." I pause. "It's my fault. I should have been keeping track of the minutes." That was a dumb mistake, and I cringe to think about how it could have wrecked everything. "I almost freaked when I saw you sitting in that classroom. Wasn't that strange to finally be there—to see it?" I ask, remembering how it was when all of my crash vision stuff fell into place.

"It was spooky and horrible." He adjusts his hands on the wheel and I notice his knuckles are all scraped up.

I think about all the things that could have happened. "One of the reasons I feel so weirdly detached from this is that I wasn't seeing it like I was last time. I mean, this time I was focused on the clues and figuring them out. I wasn't seeing body bags or dead students. I knew I had to trust you and do whatever you said. And that was really hard at first, but in the end, especially in those last seconds, I knew that was the only way to go. You were, like, navigating, and all I could do was listen and follow." I glance over at him. "And you did it."

Sawyer sighs and puts his elbow up next to the window. He scratches his head and smooths his finger over his stitches. "No, I didn't, Jules. That's the problem. I didn't stop them. They still managed to hurt people. They still managed to get attention for their hateful shit."

I shift in my seat to look at him. "Sawyer, you don't even know what you're saying. You saved almost a dozen lives! You're one guy, and you stopped this tragedy from being major. I wish I could've stopped that truck before we hit your building, or stopped it down the street before the guy had the heart attack, and saved him. But we can't do everything—the vision isn't a total fix; it's a chance to change a bad thing to something less bad. But there's no guarantee that everybody turns out fine. Come on, Sawyer," I say, my voice softening. "Don't be so hard on yourself. The vision's gone. You did what you were supposed to do. Maybe . . . maybe those people needed to go through that experience in order to become the people they're going to be, you know? Maybe that experience triggers something inside of them that will help them become great."

"And maybe it'll make them dependent on prescription drugs, or want to kill themselves." His voice is bitter.

My mouth falls open. "Are you serious right now? You think the vision gods, or whoever, gave us these chances so we can end up watching the people we save turn into drug addicts?"

"How the hell should *I* know?" he yells. "How the hell do *you* know? Are you just rationalizing it to make yourself feel better about almost getting killed?"

"I don't know what I'm doing!" I shout back at him. "I'm just trying to live my life and get through it, okay? So what if I'm rationalizing. So what? At least I'm dealing with this freak thing!"

"Just because it's over doesn't mean I'm ready to deal with it!"

We're both quiet for a long time. And then Sawyer asks in a softer voice, "When we're acting on a vision, do you ever wonder if we're invincible?"

And it's so almost funny in a superhero cartoon sort of way. But really, it's not funny at all. Because I've thought it too.

Thirty-Nine

When we come in, Trey is sitting up in the bed, his arm in a sling and a shadow of stubble on his face. "It's about time," he says. He's got the look of a stoner on his face, and I see he's got a morphine drip going. Guess Mom and Dad don't think *he'll* get addicted. Eye roll.

"You could've gotten shot a little closer to home."

He screws his face up. "Yeah, about that. What the hell happened? I don't remember anything."

Sawyer and I pull up chairs and tell him the story. Before we can finish, there's a knock on the door. A nurse pokes her head in. "Trey, a few of the students you helped save are here. They want to say thanks—is it okay if they come in?"

Trey looks at me. I nod, and Sawyer and I slide our

chairs back to get out of the way as Ben and his friend come in. I stand up and introduce Ben Galang, and Ben introduces Vernon, the guy he was with yesterday, who apparently was at the meeting, though I don't remember him.

Ben looks like he slept in his clothes. His hair is disheveled and his self-repaired glasses can't hide the dark circles under his eyes. He reaches out his hand and carefully shakes Trey's hand. "I don't know how to thank you."

Trey looks up at Ben and gives him a goofy, drugged smile. "I'm not sure why, but okay."

Ben glances at me, confused.

"We haven't quite gotten to the part of the story where Trey came in and busted up the party," I explain. "I don't think he knows what he did."

"That, and he's a little drunk on morphine," Sawyer adds.

Trey frowns. "All I remember is someone screaming 'Die, fag!' in my face, which really, you know, sucked. Then I took one look at the blood spurting out of my arm and I was like, 'Wuh-oh, check, please,' for the rest of the event." He blanches just thinking about it. "Doesn't sound very heroic to me, but whatever."

Ben brings his hand to his mouth and I can see his chin is trembling, his eyes filling up. And then he pulls his hand away and says, "The girl had a gun to my forehead.

I have a scrape here where she dug it into my skin. I was a split second away from getting my brains blown out. And then the door flew open, glass went everywhere, and the shooter was distracted." He pauses. "I got the gun off my head. And she turned and it went off. She shot you instead of me." Ben's lips quiver. He presses them together.

Clearly Trey doesn't know what to say. He opens his mouth and closes it again, and lets his head fall back against the pillows. And then he says in this hilarious Clay Aiken voice, "Well. That was right nice of me."

For a second, nobody moves, and then I snort, and everybody else sort of relaxes, and before I know it Sawyer has found more chairs and Ben is giving us updates on everybody. The girl who was shot in the abdomen, Tori, was the worst off. She made it through five hours of surgery and the doctors are cautiously hopeful. And the guy who was shot in the foot is doing okay, but the bullet shattered a bunch of bones and he won't be walking anytime soon.

Back at UC, Ben says, classes are canceled and there are counselors helping students cope. There are also reporters everywhere. Because the police caught the two alleged shooters immediately, they didn't close down the school, but a good portion of the quad is blocked off around the crime scene and a lot of students went back home. "And seriously, you guys are the unnamed heroes.

You're, like, becoming a legend," he says to all of us, but he can't stop looking at Trey, his true hero.

"Please don't give anyone our names," I find myself saying. "We don't want a bunch of reporters in our faces. We just want to, you know, get through it and move on. Our parents are sort of freaking out. I'm sure you can imagine." And then I add, "I'm only in tenth grade."

"Me too," Sawyer says. "Jules and I just want to disappear, if that's cool with you." He looks over at Trey and grins for the first time since everything happened. "Trey, on the other hand . . . he's a senior and he could really use some attention."

Trey pushes his morphine drip. "Indeed," he says, adorably loopy.

Ben smiles and turns to me. "I'm not quite sure why you guys picked this weekend to check things out at UC, or how you managed to spring to action that fast, but you really did save a lot of lives. And if you don't want your names out there, I can totally dig that. Just watch it when you're wandering around here—there are some reporters in the lobby."

"Here," Trey says, fumbling for his cell phone on the bedside table. "You should call me."

Ben turns and looks at him, a small smile still playing around his lips. "Oh, should I? What's your number?"

Trey tells him, and Ben enters it into his cell phone, and

then he takes Trey's and enters his number. "Okay," Ben says a little cautiously, "well, we'd love to have you come for a meeting. Are you seriously considering U of C? Even after what happened?"

"Oh yeah. I totally am. What's your name again?"

Ben laughs and tells him.

I frown. Trey knows U of C is a private school. Mucho big bucks. But hey . . . there's always the power of morphine to make you forget about the minor details of your life, like living above a restaurant that struggles monthly to pay its bills, and considering returning to the place where some lunatic outsider came in and fucking shot you because you're gay.

When Ben and Vernon leave, Trey looks like he's about to fall asleep. My parents will be along soon, I'm sure, so Sawyer and I go to the nurses' station to try to find out the status of the others. We learn that Tori is still in intensive care, so we're not allowed to see her, and the guy with the injured foot is asleep. So we head out a side exit and take a walk on a sunny, windy spring Monday.

I push up the stretched-out sleeve of my hoodie and look at my pasty-white arm. I was so glad to have that cast—it was like a weapon. It did way more damage than I could have done with my fist alone.

Thinking about that makes me wonder briefly what

kind of pain the shooters are in today. Trey will be proud that I kneed the guy in the meatballs. I shove my hands in my pockets and Sawyer and I walk in a somewhat awkward silence now that we're alone. I feel like we're in the middle of a fight, but we're fighting about different things.

After a while he says, "What are you going to do about your parents now that this is all over?"

And I don't know the answer, because something keeps buzzing around the back of my mind. I swat it aside. "I guess maybe try talking to them. I mean, it probably won't work, but it's actually something I haven't tried before, so who knows. We're just not really great at that." I tilt my head to look at him. "The words never come out right, you know?" He nods and I ask, "What about you?"

"I don't know."

"I hate it that you're getting hit, Sawyer."

And normally I'd expect him to get a little defensive and say something like *I don't exactly like it either.* But this time he doesn't. This time he's quiet for a long time. And then he says, "I'm leaving."

Everything inside me stops working. "What?"

"It's toxic living there. I'm moving out."

I have no pulse. My words come out as weak wisps of air, and without warning the tears pour from my eyes. "But where are you going?"

He hears the blubbering child in my voice and he turns

sharply to look at me. The hardness in his face melts and turns to surprise, then realization. "Oh, baby," he murmurs, gathering me in his arms. "God, I'm sorry—I'm not leaving you, or Chicago, or school. Just my parents and grandfather. I'm moving out. Not sure where yet, but I have a few options."

I'm flooded with relief. "You big jerk," I say, sniffling in his chest. "You don't have a fight with a girl and then say you're leaving. Even though I'm really glad you're getting away from them."

He holds me closer and I feel his breath as he laughs silently into my hair. "We had a fight? I thought that was just, you know, talking. Loudly. The Italian way."

I put my arms around his waist and raise my head to look at him. "I don't like talking loudly with you."

"I don't either. Let's not do that again." He gazes at me until I'm lost in him, and says, "Your eyes are so beautiful. I've missed them." And then we're kissing on the sidewalk in front of the University of Chicago hospital.

Forty

Five things I finally manage to get done over
spring break:
1. Buy a cell phone. Myself. I even give my parents my new number because I'm responsible
   like that
2. Call my sister to see if she's doing more making out than I am (she's not)
3. Get my job back and make it seem like I'm
   doing them a favor while Trey's out, when
   really I just kind of miss it
4. See Sawyer every day, and find out being in
   love, with no stressful visions, is way more
   fun than anything
5. Scare the hell out of Trey when I tell him

that he totally threw himself at a college boy
while under the influence of morphine

It was hilarious, that last one. I have never seen Trey
so mortified. But you know what? Ben came back to the
hospital to see Trey once more. Alone, this time, and he
stayed for over an hour. I'm just saying.

And on the morning Trey was being released, Sawyer
and I pushed him in a wheelchair to see the other victims,
and everything hit hard once again, reminding me that
solving the mystery of a vision is not the real part. The
real part is the people and the way their lives are changed
forever.

It's weird how hatred can make people do such terrible
things to other people. It kind of makes me think about
my dad. And I wonder, is his anger a form of hatred? I
think about my anger—at Sawyer's family, at the people
who want to kill other people because of who they are, at
the vision gods who put us through all of this. Is that anger
really hatred in disguise?

Or is only irrational anger actually hatred—the kind
of anger and hatred my dad has over a recipe, and toward
a family with whom he made a big mistake. Is his hatred
really aimed at them? Or is it reserved for himself, because
he's pissed about what he's done—or what he didn't do?
And does he even know that his anger affects the Angottis'

anger, and that's why Sawyer gets punched in the face by his own father?

Selfishly, I want to excuse myself, reward myself for having the proper kind of anger. The kind that helps make the world better, not the kind that festers and makes people bitter. But I don't know.

I don't know.

It's late Friday night of spring break when I run into Sawyer at the Traverse Apartments. We're delivering to different buildings this time, but I park next to him so he sees my car and waits for me when he comes out. Which he does.

"Hey," he says. "My last weekend."

I nod. He told his mother on Tuesday that he would finish the weekend to give them time to find a replacement, and that he was moving in with his cousin Kate for a while, maybe forever, and taking a part-time job at the Humane Society.

He says his mother cried. And that makes me furious. I think, where the fuck are the tears before it's too late, you moms? Where are they? Why does it have to go this far before you let yourself break? But I don't say anything. That's my own battle, and my family is walking on eggshells until somebody (me) decides it's time to deal with it (just . . . not yet).

"How's Rowan?"

"She had a blast once our parents calmed down and got distracted with Trey. But she said she wasn't sure it was worth lying about. Now she's the one Dad's eyeing, asking her if she's pregnant." I laugh a little, but my mind is elsewhere, on my dad, wondering things I don't want to wonder but I know soon I'm going to have to ask him about. I lean against my car and pull on Sawyer's hoodie strings. "You doing all right?" I ask. "After the vision, I mean."

He shrugs. "I think so. Considering."

"Trey tried to be hilarious today," I tell him. "He came into my room this morning and told me he had a vision."

Sawyer's eyes open wide. "That's so not funny."

"My heart totally sank—I mean, I almost started bawling, you know? I don't know if I could do this again." I look at him hard.

"Oh, God," he says. He looks away, picturing it, I suppose. He shakes his head. "I really am glad that we had a chance to save people, but I'll tell you what—I can eliminate police officer and firefighter from my list of things I want to be when I grow up."

"I just hope . . . ," I begin. "No. Never mind."

He narrows his eyes and focuses in on me. "What," he says slowly.

I shrug. Bite my lip. "I mean, obviously I had a vision and somehow I passed it to you. And now, who knows? Maybe it's done. Or maybe . . . it's not."

Sawyer grips the back of his neck and leans against his car door. "What are you saying?" he says, like he knows what I'm saying.

"I'm just . . . I don't know. What if you got your vision because I saved you, and now you saved people, and one of them is having a vision, only we don't know it."

"Oh my God, Jules," Sawyer says, and I can see he's straining not to raise his voice. "This is not our problem. Are you kidding me? You are not responsible for saving the whole fucking world. Besides, where'd you get your vision from, then?"

I look down at the pavement. And I wonder, not for the first time, if my father's illness is responsible for this. And my grandfather's, too. Maybe these visions have been a Demarco family curse for generations, and I just unleashed the curse to the rest of the world. Back when I was feeling sick out of my mind, seeing that explosion and Sawyer in a body bag, I almost asked Dad if he'd ever had a vision. Maybe I should have. Because what if he's been having a vision for years, but he doesn't know what to do? And what if my grandfather had a vision too, and it got so bad that he killed himself—because it was the only way he knew to be free of it? Maybe the Angottis actually have very little to do with my family's history of depression, and it's been *this* all along. What if all the visions started with Demarcos and stayed with Demarcos, and none of us figured out how to get them to stop, so the visions festered inside of people until it ruined them. And then I came along and stopped mine. And by stopping my vision, I passed the curse to someone I saved. And by stopping Sawyer's . . . Well. I just have to find out.

"It started with me," I say. I glance up at Sawyer. "But that doesn't really matter, does it? It doesn't change anything. It's what happens next that matters. We're talking about people's lives—what if Trey hadn't helped me save you? What if Trey and I hadn't helped you with the shooting? I can't let some traumatized shooting victim handle the next thing alone." I shrug. "I can't. I unleashed the beast."

Sawyer stares at me. And then slowly he shakes his head, and I can tell his mind is made up. "No way," he says. "No way."

One look at his set jaw and I know he's not going to change his mind. I hold his gaze a moment more, and then I nod and attempt a smile, because this is not his battle. He's a victim of the Demarco curse, like everybody else.

"Okay," I say. "I understand." I pull the keys from my pocket, and then I reach up and caress Sawyer's cheek, pull him close. Kiss him until the tension between us melts away. And when we pull apart, I tell him I love him. And that I have to do this—I have to find out if anybody else is having a vision. And if someone is, I have to help. That's the way it's going to be, that's my responsibility, and I'm going to do it. Invincible or not, I started this, and I'm in it until I see a way out.

He just stares at me like I've lost my mind again.

I hope I can't find anyone with a vision. With all my heart, I hope this mess ends with us, but frankly, I doubt it does. And I can't rest until I know for sure.

When I get home it's late. Rowan's fast asleep. I lie on my bed, eyes closed, trying to picture the music room. Trying to count the people in there. Wondering where to start, how to track them all down. What to say when I do. Eventually I get up and find Trey watching late-night TV in the living room. He's got his bad arm in a sling, the other hand in a bowl of popcorn.

"Hey. You have Ben's phone number, right?" I ask.

He shoves popcorn in his mouth and nods, eyes narrowing. "Why?" he asks, his mouth full.

"I need it."

He stares at me, chewing slowly. He swallows and pauses the TV show. "Why?" he says again, suspicious.

I drop my gaze, studying a stack of board games, trying to decide if I should tell him. Finally, I say in a softer voice, "I just do. I need to make sure nobody new is . . . affected."

His hand drops to his lap. His eyes close, and he sighs heavily. "Shit," he says. "You gotta be kidding me."

I stare at the floor.

He sits up, his voice suddenly concerned, like he's just realizing what I'm saying. "Wait. If Sawyer passed the vision to Ben," Trey says, "I swear I'll shoot you both in the face."

"I know. Just give me the number. I'll call him in the morning."

He hesitates a moment more, like he can't believe this is happening, then sets the popcorn bowl on a pile of magazines next to the chair and pulls his phone from his pocket. He forwards Ben's contact info to my phone. "Try not to sound like a total psycho. And, you know. Don't make me look bad."

"Yeah, sure. No problem."

He attempts a reassuring smile, but his eyes are worried when I say good night.

At three in the morning my cell phone buzzes, and at first I think it's a dream. I finally wake up enough to answer. It's Sawyer. "Hey," I whisper, propping myself up on my elbow. "What's up?"

The line is quiet, but I know he's there. I can almost feel his chest move as he breathes, see his earnest eyes adorned with those ropy lashes, sense the trepidation in his voice before he speaks. And all he does is whisper three simple, beautiful words that I've come to love hearing.

"Okay," he says. "I'm in."

About the Author

Lisa McMann is the author of the *New York Times* bestelling Wake trilogy, *Cryer's Cross*, *Dead to You*, the Visions series, and the middle-grade dystopian fantasy series The Unwanteds. She lives with her family in the Phoenix area. Read more about Lisa and find her blog through her website at LISAMcMANN.com or, better yet, find her on Facebook (facebook.com/mcmannfan) or follow her on Twitter (twitter.com/lisa_mcmann).